PRAISE FOR
INGRID WINTERBACH

"In her latest novel, Ingrid Winterbach is at her best: complex, funny, smart, mischievous, and without equal."—*Beeld*

"Winterbach's writing sets the mood brilliantly, and she pitches her blend of characters perfectly to create an uneasy, occasionally frightening feel to her narrative."—*Belletrista*

"An exquisite book, an essential voice."—Antjie Krog

"A grim, dark, unrelenting book—an exhaustive survey of the sensations of war, from headlice and crippling thirst to grief, suffering, and madness."—*Words Without Borders*

"What makes this novel and its fresh English-language publication so timely is that its themes have become uncomfortably familiar."
—*Austin Chronicle*

"This is an extraordinary story from an extraordinary writer. . . . If you haven't experienced the mind of Ingrid Winterbach yet, she is a writer who clings to your soul."—*Pretoria News*

"This unforgettable novel establishes Ingrid Winterbach as one of the most important novelists writing in Afrikaans."—Thys Human

THE ELUSIVE MOTH

Ingrid Winterbach

Translated from the Afrikaans
by Iris Gouws & the Author

OPEN LETTER
LITERARY TRANSLATIONS FROM THE UNIVERSITY OF ROCHESTER

Library of Congress Cataloging-in-Publication Data: Available upon request.
ISBN-13: 978-1-934824-77-1 / ISBN-10: 1-934824-77-1

Printed on acid-free paper in the United States of America.

Text set in Bembo, an old-style serif typeface based upon face cuts by
Francesco Griffo that were first printed in 1496.

Design by N. J. Furl.
Butterfly designed by Evan MacDonald from the Noun Project

Open Letter is the University of Rochester's nonprofit, literary translation press:
Lattimore Hall 411, Box 270082, Rochester, NY 14627

www.openletterbooks.org

For Evelyn Coetzee

And to the memory of
Iris Marguerite Gouws
(1942-1998)

THE ELUSIVE MOTH

Every person ought to be very attentive and listen for the stroke, before he opens the door of a billiard room
—*Horace Lindrum:* Snooker, billiards and pool

CHAPTER 1

LONG AGO, Karolina Ferreira had had a dream: of a promenade by the sea with a row of palm trees growing down the centre, and the body of a man, hacked in two, with blood spurting from it.

She recalled this dream as Basil knelt down, taking the leaf of a plant between his fingers.

He was of medium height, strongly built, and his skin was an unvaried shade of brown. His eyes were clear, his head was striking: its proportions unusually harmonious.

"You can use these leaves to prepare a cure for blood spurting from a wound," he said. "But only if it spurts quite strongly. If it is pumped away with every beat of the heart. There are other kinds of bleeding that are slower—after childbirth, for instance—and then the blood is darker."

This was their first morning out in the veld, and it was very hot. They had arrived there the day before: at the dorp Voorspoed, in the Free State. They wore hats. The spruit was dry. Even the willows seemed to sag. The grass was brown. Karolina's head was ringing with the heat. Her temples ached. Several hours of intense effort and concentration had left her feeling faint.

Every now and again Basil would kneel down. He found small plants, tiny flowers, insects, dry bones, and land shells among the tufts of dry grass. He explained the properties of each of them.

What a strange pair they were, thought Karolina.

"And this," said Basil, pointing to a small, yellow flower, "is what's given to someone who cannot reconcile himself to dying. Should such a person take this, he would let go." He opened his hand. Karolina gazed into his clear eyes.

Bleeding and dying. That's it, she realised. Against excessive bleeding, against blood that spurted. Against laborious dying. Pity those who had no such means of comfort.

They sat down near the dry course of the spruit, under a willow tree, right up against the trunk where the shade was deepest. Would the crabs have survived, she wondered, it was so very dry.

Karolina observed a smallish, damp spot in the sand before her. The ants were milling around it energetically.

"Someone was here before us," said Basil.

"How do you know?" asked Karolina.

"Footprints, flattened grass, some kind of moisture," Basil replied.

Karolina leant forward. Took a closer look.

"Who could it have been?" she asked.

"We'll see them," he said. "On the way back."

They ate hard-boiled eggs. Sandwiches they had bought at the Springbok Café. They had tea from a Thermos. Tiny scraps of egg fell to the ground.

"More food for the ants," said Karolina.

They walked back to town. They walked slowly, since it was very hot. First a long way across the veld, and then down End Street which ran parallel to the cemetery.

The town was dead quiet. Everybody had retired behind drawn curtains. The hour of the scarab. Much too hot to be out on the street.

She suggested they should cut through the cemetery, it seemed cooler there. When they had covered a small distance, they saw two people sitting on a bench near a cypress tree. A man and a woman.

"There they are," said Basil.

Karolina did not want to stare openly.

It was impossible to place the man, he did not seem to be one of the locals—something charismatic about him? The woman was

6

heart-rendingly beautiful. Poignantly beautiful, and distressed. Pro-foundly distressed, it seemed. Undoubtedly a pair of lovers, there could be no other explanation, thought Karolina. But why banish their love to this remote corner?

"What do you think?" she asked Basil as they walked down Stie-beuel Street to the hotel.

"Lovers," he said. "If they're seen together, it'll be tickets. The stakes are high."

When they arrived at the hotel, he spat out the remnants of a leaf he had been chewing on.

"Have you ever seen a more beautiful woman?" Karolina asked.

Basil thought about it briefly.

"Yes," he said. "I know one woman who is more beautiful."

Two men sat at a small table on the long, cool stoep that extended along the front of the hotel. They were drinking beer. They were watching Karolina and Basil with some interest. Both men were tall, she observed in passing. One of them had a noticeably rusty complexion and wore glasses; the other had short, dark hair, and a wry, uneasy smile.

Basil took one look at them. "I'll put my money on the red one," he said as he and Karolina passed through the hotel entrance.

As they crossed the dusky hotel lounge to go to the dining room, they saw a burly blond man, motionless in an easy chair. The beer on the table before him remained untouched.

"He's taking it badly, but he's a gentleman," said Basil.

"What money?" Karolina asked as they were about to study the menu. (She did not often frequent hotels.)

Basil gestured with his head.

"You'll see for yourself," he said.

After lunch Basil returned to his lodgings with Mr. Quiroga the Argentinian, who had a house in the upper part of town.

Karolina went upstairs to her room. She passed through the re-markable reception area, which was pure baroque—imported by lord knows who into a region renowned for its sheep and maize. The reception desk, the baldachin above it, and the staircase balusters were of dark oak, elaborately carved with ornate scrolls, leaves, flower motifs, and cherubs; sensuously curving and swelling forms. She went up the stairs, the handrail smooth as satin under the palm of her hand. She walked down the long corridor to her room. The carpet was worn. No sign here of the baroque fantasies and excesses of the reception area.

Her room was located at an angle over the hotel entrance, it looked out on the main street; it was cool and dim. She stood before the mirror. Her eyes stared back darkly. The dark eyebrows were heavy. Her shoulders had lost their soft, feminine curve. Her skin was pale, despite the natural darkness of her complexion. Her dark hair was badly cut. She looked like someone in the process of becoming. Unfinished. Incomplete.

She sat down on her bed; she looked at the palm of her hand. On their way here the previous day she and Basil had reached the outskirts of a small town towards sunset, and had stopped to fill up with petrol.

There was a Wimpy next to the garage; there was a circular patch of grass directly opposite, and on it—as if on a little island—a caravan was parked. A woman who could see into the future offered her services. The sky was gold and fire, the sun a fiery ball on the horizon. Karolina entered the caravan by the spectacular glow of its setting.

Once inside, she deposited a twenty rand note in a frilly dish and sat down facing the woman across a small, portable folding table. The woman turned on a tiny light, and took Karolina's hand in hers. Her hair was a gilded nest reaching up to the roof—a bird could have flown up from it. The interior overflowed with mirrors, ornaments, shells, coils, reflections; every surface and corner crammed in rococo abundance.

The woman opened Karolina's hand and looked into the warm, somewhat sweaty palm. She slipped into a light trance. "I see," she said, "I see here . . ."

What did she see?

She saw a man who would love Karolina forever, and she saw a woman, a close friend, who would never let her down.

When Karolina emerged from the caravan the sun had just gone down. Its moment of gilded glory had passed and she and Basil resumed their journey.

KAROLINA FELT TIRED after the journey of the day before and after the long walk in the veld with Basil that morning. It was hot. She fell asleep. Blood coursed slowly through her warm, sleeping body.

She woke up at four o'clock. She rose and took a walk. More than twenty-five years ago she had been more familiar with this town. Her father had done some of his research here and her family had occasionally spent their summer holidays here in a large, cool, rented house.

The town was remarkably unchanged. It had a simple, rectangular layout. The long main street extended as far as the church. The other streets ran parallel to the main street, or at right angles to it. The business centre had apparently not expanded much beyond a couple of blocks on either side of the main street. None of the original buildings had been demolished. The concrete pavements outside the shop fronts were still wide, with generous verandahs on slender cast-iron posts or sturdier cement pillars. But the Oasis Café was no longer there—in its place was a stationery shop. Nortjé's Chemist was now the Village Pharmacy (a few dusty Christmas gifts remained on display in a corner). Had Mr. Nortjé died, or was he retired? (She still remembered him.) And what might have become of Mevrou? Besides the two cafés and Nortjé's Chemist Karolina could not recall any other shops, but Pep Stores and Spar were recent additions, as were the chain stores Milady's and Foschini, and another chemist some distance away on the other side of the street. She had noticed this morning that many of the streets were still not tarred, and some of the houses in the upper part of town looked surprisingly familiar. She saw that the small Avbob funeral parlour in one of the side streets had been painted pink, but she could not locate the municipal swimming pool, where her father had taken her and her sister swimming as young girls.

Emotionally she had long since withdrawn from this place, there was nothing here to which she might attach herself now. She no longer knew anyone here. The town with its streets of fine brown gravel and peace on earth had disappeared. There was a different feel to it now.

Massive thunderclouds were gathering behind the church. A policeman came round a corner, wearing blue Crimplene (or Terylene) trousers; some synthetic fabric that stretched tightly over the crotch. He had a walkie-talkie in his hand. For a moment he stared at her fixedly.

She crossed the street to go to the Rendezvous Café for tea. She was filled with a sense of anticipation and slight foreboding—she could no longer clearly picture the interior of the café. The front part, she saw, resembled all cafés across the country nowadays, but the tearoom at the back belonged to a previous era.

There was an icy draught in the room in spite of the heat. Some forlorn Christmas decorations were suspended from the ceiling, which was very high, old, and very ornate. She sat down at a table immediately behind the wooden partition that separated this area from the front. Someone was sitting at a table in the opposite corner. It was one of the men who had sat on the hotel stoep earlier on, the one on whom Basil had put his money. He nodded a greeting. She nodded in return. He went back to his reading. A Christmas decoration was lifted by the breeze. The proprietress took Karolina's order. There was a clamour from the kitchen to the right. The woman returned with her tea; they were preparing for a wedding that was to take place in the evening, she said.

Karolina found it hard to drink her tea unselfconsciously. She was uncomfortably aware of the man in the opposite corner. She did not wish to stare at him openly, but she wanted to try and see what Basil had meant. What was he reading? A book with a red cover like burning flames. It matched the red glow emitted by his skin (even in the semidark it emitted this glow); it seemed as if he had had too much sun recently. When she glanced in his direction once more, he was looking at her too. She finished her tea quickly, rose, nodded a greeting, paid, and walked out.

The sky was growing steadily darker, more menacing, a deeper shade of blue in the south, to the left of the church at the top end of the main street. The spectacle of the dramatically darkening sky soon came to dominate the town. This region, too, could do with rain—the drought was tightening its noose.

Karolina walked back to the hotel quickly to avoid being caught in the rain.

Along the way she saw several handmade posters tied to the street lights, saying:

> The Delarey and Beyers
> Theatrical Company presents:
> THE JEALOUS HUSBAND
> Based on a classic hit.
> In the town hall on Saturday night.
> All welcome. Refreshments.

When she arrived at the hotel, she saw that the dark cloud formations behind the church steeple were moving away, the sky had turned a murky grey. From her vantage point in front of the hotel, at the lower end of the main street, with the church at the very far end, the town took on a familiar appearance for a few moments and Karolina was overcome with an inexplicable longing.

The last time she had been here, she had still possessed a sleepy innocence—though even then, at that youthful age, she had known the classification and taxonomy of the twenty-nine orders.

AFTER DINNER Karolina went to the ladies' bar. She had only just taken a seat at the bar counter when a shortish, dark-haired man approached her, a drink in his hand.

"Pol Habermaut," he said. "Lawyer," and shook her hand.

He pulled up a bar stool, and sat down beside her. He studied her attentively, taking his time, tilting his head slightly in order to observe her better. His hair and face were drenched with perspiration. His head was as sleek as an otter's. His skin had the texture of an aquatic animal. He swayed to and fro slightly.

"Have we met before in what is generally known as the New Dispensation?" he asked.

"No," she said.

He asked about the purpose of her visit to the town.

She told him that she studied insects, and that she was doing research on a particular moth species that was found mainly in the area.

He studied her at length once again. He licked his lips. "I shudder at the thought of all you may discover here," he said.

"I hope I do," she said.

She surveyed the room. Apart from the bar counter with its high stools, there were easy chairs in green and maroon imitation leather, arranged round low, round tables. There were animal trophies on the walls, potted plants on wrought-iron stands in the corners, and a large zebra skin on one wall. The room was cosily lit by small lights on the walls and at the bar.

There were not many people around, probably because it was a weeknight. Karolina's gaze fell upon a man who sat in the farthest corner of the room, over to the left. She observed him closely for a few seconds.

"Who is that?" she asked Pol, indicating the man with a movement of her head.

Pol brought his head closer to hers. He spoke softly, confidentially, in a subdued tone.

"Our magistrate," he said.

He gave her a grave, conspiratorial look.

"Not a lad whose personal affairs we want to meddle in," he said.

"I see," she said.

The magistrate was a stout, middle-aged man. He was sucking, or perhaps biting, the rim of his glass. His other hand was spread open on the armrest of the chair. He did not appear to respond to what the man opposite him was saying.

"Some of the lads here are greatly burdened with cares," said Pol, once more giving her a meaningful look. She looked back—deep into his aquatic eyes. She liked him.

"I see," she said.

He took leave of her and joined his friends at a table to her right, in the corner directly opposite the magistrate. Shortly afterwards he launched into the first song of the evening. He had a deep, sonorous voice, and the ability to give a suggestive turn to the most innocent song.

Presently Basil entered the ladies' bar; they had arranged to meet here.

"How're things, Basil?" she asked.

"Not too bad," replied Basil, looking neither right nor left.

"That man in the corner there," she said, motioning cautiously towards the magistrate, "what do you make of him?"

Basil poured his beer calmly, then took a sidelong glance.

"He pisses a forked green stream," said Basil.

"Oh," said Karolina.

Basil took a swig.

"Probably rejected by the mother at an early age," he said. "Unquenchable thirst. Iron constitution. Irritable. Critical. Malicious. Manipulative. Predisposition to anal warts. Migraine lodged in the left eye, as if a nail has been driven into it."

Basil gazed serenely before him.

"Do you know him?" asked Karolina.

"No," said Basil.

"So?"

"So?"

"How do you know these things?" she asked.

"Anyone can do it," he said, "there are no tricks to it."

Karolina hesitated momentarily.

"Why do you put your money on the red one?" she asked.

"You'll see for yourself," he said.

Every time she looked in Pol's direction, he was looking at her, nodding meaningfully, before launching into a new song in his resonant voice.

Karolina suggested that she and Basil go next door, to see what was happening in the snooker room.

As she entered, Karolina felt the hairs along her spine and the back of her neck stand on end. A room filled with strange vibrations, a place where one could go mad and commit a crime, where one could lose one's head and one's good judgement, and be at the mercy of the collusions of one's neighbour as well as one's own unfathomable drives. A place that might unexpectedly activate the links in a chain of old memories. A congenial place, cosy.

One side of the room was occupied by a half-size snooker table. The remainder was taken up by cane and imitation leather easy chairs. There were antelope heads on the walls (as in the ladies' bar), advertisements for beer, and framed photographs. The walls were painted a strange yellow—probably caused by the reflection from the large light over the green surface of the snooker table. On the floor a threadbare, olive-green wall-to-wall carpet. The room was considerably lighter than the ladies' bar.

Here, too, there were few visitors tonight.

A man in uniform, who had been leaning over the table, straightened up when they entered. It was the policeman in blue she had encountered that afternoon. Now without his cap. He had narrow, oriental eyes and muscular forearms; he gazed at her briefly before returning to the game. When he had played his shot, he put the cue down, wiped his palms on his trousers, and approached them with outstretched hand.

"Kieliemann," he said, "Lieutenant. Pleased to meet you." Inscrutable.

He introduced them to the other players round the table and to the other people in the room. There was a Sergeant Frikkie Visser, a Sergeant Yap Buytendach; a Mr. Maritz and a Mr. Retief (who looked like members of the FAK); there were two lacklustre teachers

14

in a corner: a Mr. Abel Kriek and a Mr. Tiny Botha, and a travelling salesman with a strange name (Karolina had seen him in the dining room at lunchtime).

They were met with various intonations, inflexions and degrees of suspicion and fake Afrikaner cordiality, but no one took them seriously. Not Karolina, since she was a woman, and not Basil, because his surname was September.

At that moment a man entered by the rear door, the one leading to the toilets. Emerged from the shadows, so to speak. He was exceptionally tall and exceptionally pale.

Karolina hesitated for a moment before shaking his extended hand, during which she took account of a few facts. His hand was icy cold, the palm sweaty.

"Captain Gert Els," he said. Pale eyes, she noted.

Karolina and Basil turned down an invitation from Lieutenant Kieliemann to join in the game. Later, Karolina indicated, maybe later in the week. She motioned unobtrusively to Basil—let's get out of here as quickly as possible.

"Let's go out on the stoep for a drink," she said softly.

"What did it look like to you in there, Basil?" she asked when they were sitting outside with the cool night air on their cheeks. They had taken the table where the two men had sat earlier that day.

Basil simply laughed.

"The same as everywhere else around these parts," he said. "No better, no worse."

"What did you make of the captain?" she asked.

Basil gave a small shrug. "A man who finds it hard to restrain himself," he said.

"I had a fright in there," said Karolina.

A small shudder passed through her. A little windy outside?

"I don't trust him. For a moment I thought he was someone else. Someone I knew a long time ago."

Basil looked at her fixedly for a moment. As if she had said more about herself than about the man in there.

ON FRIDAY MORNING Karolina found a finger in the veld. Or something that closely resembled a finger. A strange vegetative growth, white and rootlike. Basil studied the unusual object carefully. Then he put it into a brown paper bag to take home with him. Karolina recalled a dream she had had the previous night of black stones and black locusts.

They were both well equipped for the veld. Karolina was doing research on the distribution and breeding patterns of the moth species *Hebdomophruda crenilinea*. (A small, inconspicuous moth, difficult to find, pale as a shroud.) Basil was in search of a variety of things. He helped Mr. Quiroga the Argentinian to prepare his remedies. They would spend months, and in some cases years, he told her, preparing some of these remedies from the various raw ingredients.

The moth in question was found mainly in this region. Close on a hundred years before, Boer and Brit had roamed the area freely. The province had been a contested terrain. Women, children, and blacks had been forcibly moved around in great clouds of dust like herds of animals. The earth had been burnt down—the devastated soil yielded little afterwards. The vegetation and insect life had suffered a huge setback—in many places for kilometres on end not a flower, not a plant, not a tuft of grass remained, not a stone had been left unturned. The surface of the earth had been reduced to dust by thousands of larger and smaller-hoofed animals moving across it repeatedly for months on end.

It was dry in this area now, and had been for a long time. Karolina was researching the survival strategies of this species of moth under these extreme circumstances.

They walked back to town before lunch. Once more they chose the route past the cemetery. It was so hot it seemed that the cypresses were vibrating; they cast no shadow. No sign of the lovers. They arrived back in the cool, baroque reception area of the hotel tired, dusty, and hungry, and had lunch in the dining room with the six painted panels. These panels depicted events from the historyof the land—confrontations between Boer and Brit, between black and white.

Karolina rested in the afternoon. She had a dream: a stain appeared. It was wet and it spread like blood.

When she woke up, she looked at the palm of her hand. The woman had seen two people in it: a man who would love her forever, and a woman who would never let her down. The sky had indeed been a fiery red when she had entered that caravan. She thought of the white root finger Basil had placed in the paper bag. A bizarre find. She thought of the dance that would be held in the hotel the following night (she had seen it advertised in the reception area). She thought of Pol, of the members of the local police force she had met in the snooker room (she thought of Gert Els in particular), of the magistrate, and of the lovers who had gazed at each other with such passion and intensity in the cemetery, and she thought of her own life.

She knew that her ability to analyse and interpret facts in the field of entomology was unfortunately of no use when it came to understanding people and human relationships.

ON FRIDAY NIGHT she had a dream. A man appeared who had courted her a long time ago, who had made love to her, had known her carnally. First he reviled her, then he confessed, hopelessly lecherous, down on his hands and knees. Repeatedly. In a scene of obscene, improper, indecorous lewdness he made a public confession. Down on his knees and tearful, in a chaos of abundant flesh. Improperly, triumphantly endowed. She woke up in confusion. Could it be he, wherever he might find himself now, could he be the one who still loved her? Highly unlikely. Even then he had hardly been capable of love. Unlikely that his capacity would have increased with the passage of time and in her absence.

Now they began to parade before her night after night—the men she had known, had desired in some way or other, had hung her heart on; had indifferently surrendered her body to, no matter whose unrestrained pleasure it served. Like show horses they appeared. Each one in turn. Every single one of them, from the time before her self-imposed celibacy.

She dreamt about the man to whom she had given her heart most completely. He was a shadow of his former self. Not even that. He lay abandoned, dead, his throat cut. A woman was looking on, her clothes were torn, she was clutching an expensive handbag made of crocodile skin as if it might be the last remnant of an honourable, or even a plausible life.

SHE WOKE UP early on Saturday morning. She had to buy a few small items in town. People were dancing on the street corners, thronging together. (They had probably been driven in from the farms in lorry loads that morning.) A lively disco-noise was coming from the ghetto blasters. Karolina was excited, but restrained herself. In the Rendezvous Café she ordered tea, massaging her calves while waiting for her order. She did not find the dismal interior depressing today. A dusty warmth penetrated the cool, dim interior of the room. On the other side of the wide windowsills, painted a rich cream colour, small groups of women chatted on the pavements. Karolina did not understand the language they spoke, but she liked the sounds, they were soothing, familiar.

She had just started drinking her tea when the man Basil had put his money on, entered the room. This time he came straight to her table. He introduced himself as Jess Jankowitz, and asked if she would mind if he joined her. Did she come here for tea every day, and how long did she intend to stay in town? he asked.

She did not mind if he joined her, she came here for a cup of tea every day, and she would be staying on indefinitely, she said.

The man Jess was shy. Behind his glasses his eyes were self-conscious. He had heavy eyelids that gave him a somewhat slow, lazy appearance. His skin was still emitting a red glow; it was burnt a deep copper, and his face, forearms and hands were slightly freckled. His hair, thinning in front, was a deep, rusty brown in the nape of his neck.

His hand rested on the same book as the other day, with the red cover like burning flames. It was a long, slim hand, freckly, covered in reddish blond fur.

18

"What are you reading?" she asked.

"Oh," he said, "a kind of manual."

"What sort of manual?" she asked.

He gave a little laugh, lowered his gaze. "To help free oneself of false perceptions," he said. He spoke hesitantly, his eyes not clearly visible behind the reflection of his glasses. "They're meditation techniques. To help rid you of things that obscure your understanding."

The owner came in with Jess's tea. Outside the wide, cool windowsill the women's clear voices were audible. It was hot outside, and dry. A permanent cloud of dust hung in the air.

They sat in silence for a few moments.

"What does one meditate on?" she asked.

"On many things," he said. "On mortality, on death. Other people's death. One's own death." He gave a small shrug. "There are many forms of meditation."

"A worthwhile practice, by the sound of it," said Karolina.

"It is," said Jess.

He asked what had brought her to this town.

She gave a brief account of her research on moths in the area. Did he live in the town, was he employed here? she asked.

No, he said, he lived in the Western Cape. He was here on sabbatical. He knew the town well, his grandparents had lived here.

What was his area of research?

His area of research was economics, he said. He was working on theories of macro-economic equilibrium.

They finished their tea. She rose to leave. He would walk with her, he said, he still had something to do in town.

When he stood up straight, she saw for the first time how tall he really was. And not slight—his body suggested a great solidity—in spite of the slender hands and the delicately tapering fingers. And the strange glow as if he were burning on the inside, as if one might be able to warm oneself at him. And the frecklishness, of all things. And the evasive gaze and the heavy eyelids. His body in all likelihood also covered in bronze fur, she thought involuntarily. Not the sort of man she would have fantasised about in her youth and during the times of foolishness after that.

When they parted, he asked if she had plans for the evening. Yes, she had, she said, but she did not tell him that she intended to go dancing.

ON SATURDAY AFTERNOON she rested. She imagined she could hear the wind rustling in the bluegums somewhere. When she woke up, she painted her toenails. She did this carefully, putting cotton wool plugs between the toes. Then she began to warm up. Since she did not trust the wooden floor (with worn carpet), she did so on top of the bed. (Which was fortunately exceptionally well sprung). She moved up and down on the spot at a terrific pace. Her hair was tied back tightly. She was dripping with perspiration. Afterwards she massaged warm oil into her legs, took a shower and put on her blue dress. In the mirror she saw a woman who seemed to reach out to the world with limitless confidence.

When she heard the music start up, she went downstairs. At a glance she noticed that the magistrate was in his place in the ladies' bar. From the snooker room a great boisterousness was already audible. She walked round the building to the eastern stoep adjoining the dining room—through the window she had a glimpse of tables and chairs stacked against the back wall. She sat down at a small table and ordered a glass of orange squash. It was pleasantly cool on the stoep. A considerable number of people were sitting here; some had already started to dance inside. It seemed the Saturday night dance drew a great many of the local inhabitants.

She recognised a few of the men she had met in the snooker room on Thursday night. Sergeant Boet Visagie and spouse were there, as were Sergeant Yap Buytendach and spouse. The two FAK individuals were accompanied by their fiancées (the girls did not look like spouses). The two lacklustre teachers and their wives were seated at another table. The young wife of the duller of the pair (Mr. Kriek?) had a tiny head as if her skull had gradually shrivelled up during the years she had spent in the presence of her dreary husband.

Lieutenant Kieliemann, Pol and Sergeant Frikkie were not present. They were probably in the snooker room—without their spouses. She would have to see. It seemed there were those who played snooker, those who danced, those who sat in the ladies' bar, and those who played snooker and danced. There were probably more, but those were the most important categories.

Karolina sat quietly; she gazed straight ahead of her, she drank her orange squash; she knew and obeyed the rules of the game.

A small group of men was sitting at a table a short distance away, somewhat separate from the rest. They were laughing and drinking beer. She expected the first action to come from this quarter. (Even now the beat of the music inside seemed unbearably inviting.)

She was right. One of the men got up, approached her, introduced himself as Kolyn (nothing more and nothing less), and asked her to dance with him. A man with a dark Voortrekker beard.

He led her inside by the elbow. Below the painted panels high up on the walls and the slowly-revolving ceiling fans, he took her in his arms, and for the duration of the dance she voluntarily submitted her will to his.

If the Kolyn fellow had noticed anything unusual, he showed no sign of it. When Karolina returned to her room exhausted late that night, she thought she could consider herself lucky. It did not always happen that she found the best dancer so early in the evening, or even at all, at such an occasion. She might do much worse than dance with him every Saturday night.

Unfortunately and inevitably she might also do better. Karolina was an exceptional dancer, in addition to her considerable ability in the field of entomology.

CHAPTER 2

KAROLINA FERREIRA and Basil September would go out into the veld every morning. She to gather information pertaining to the moths, he to look for and collect herbs and other ingredients. After lunch she would rest, then she would write up and expand on the morning's field observations. It was early January, extremely hot—almost the hottest time of the year—and dry. When she was unable to sleep, she would merely lie there, thinking about the morning's finds, or about the development of her argument, or about the things Basil had shown or told her. Or she would think about people she had known. Or about certain situations she had found herself in. Or she would allow her associations to proliferate unchecked—attending to each as it arose. Sometimes she would be struck by an idea that seemed to descend on her out of the blue: an insight, a fantasy, an intuition, an intimation.

Occasionally they would play snooker after dinner in the evening.

Pol and the magistrate were in the ladies' bar almost every night, whereas Lieutenant Kieliemann, Sergeants Boet Visagie, Yap Buytendach, Frikkie Visser, and a small band of regulars seemed to hang out in the snooker room.

It was not for nothing that Lieutenant Kieliemann had been watering at the mouth since the very first evening of their acquaintance. While he was a man who remained perfectly impassive in the presence of others, he soon—the minute he found himself alone with Karolina—made his intentions known to her. On Tuesday night she encountered him on her way to the toilet, in the tiny corridor off the rear entrance to the snooker room (the very entrance at which Gert Els had made his first appearance).

He pressed her up against the wall and tried to kiss her.

Somewhat taken aback, she tried to break free from his embrace, but he was both persistent and strong.

"Please," he breathed in her neck.

Without a word she managed to disengage herself. She rushed to the ladies' toilet. On her return to the snooker room, Kieliemann looked up as she entered, but showed not the slightest sign that something had just passed between them. She sat down next to Basil on the cane seat.

"Kieliemann," she said in an undertone. "What's his case?"

"Schizoid disposition and a tendency towards fetishism," Basil said, "cruel to his subordinates, submissive to his superiors. Cool exterior, burning interior. Excessive sexual fantasies."

Next door in the ladies' bar Pol was singing "Spring with her Magic Wand." Karolina drank whisky and kept an eye on the players. Kieliemann played viciously (he had an unerring eye and a lethal aim); Frikkie Visser panicked easily; Boet Visagie's movements lacked coordination; Yap Buytendach's game was grim and determined (he was much too intent on winning); Basil was an impressive player (this must be the only reason they tolerate his presence here, she thought). Karolina enjoyed the game, but still had much to learn.

Presently Pol's sleek otter's head appeared round the door. He caught sight of her, smiled fondly, came swimming towards her, glass in hand, and settled down beside her. He fixed a searching, watery gaze on her. His eyes were the colour of swamp water, the whites almost invisible. He gave off a great, steamy heat. He wiped the sweat from his forehead with a handkerchief. He was singing the closing bars of his last song, softly, close to her ear. "And everywhere her dainty footprints lie," he sang, "the tender verdant grass doth rise, the verdant grass doth ri-hise."

He paused, tilting his head to one side to take a better look at her.

"Tell me," he said, "have you found anything of importance yet?"

"No," she said, "the moths are elusive. That's why they're so good at surviving in extreme conditions."

Pol gave her a long, penetrating look.

"I shudder to think of the awesome powers of this moth," he said, and shuddered visibly. A violent tremor passed through his body. A faraway look appeared in his eyes.

Once more he directed a watery gaze at Karolina.

"Do you know the history of this region?" he asked.

"Not really," she replied.

"Right here," he said, pausing dramatically, "a major campaign was launched by one of our great generals. A mere stone's throw away, just the other side of town."

Pol took a huge swig from his glass.

"I shudder at the thought of certain fateful moments in the history of our land," he said.

Karolina leaned over so that their heads almost touched.

"I thought you might tell me something more about these people," she said.

Pol gave her a meaningful look.

"Most of the lads here tonight are burdened with cares," he said. "They hardly know the extent of their sorrows," he added blithely. With these words he said goodbye and went off to the ladies' bar, where he joined his friends in a fresh round of song.

> The joys of spring are all a-round,
> Bright buds and fra-grant blooms a-bound,
> The smi-ling sun, the gen-tle rain,
> The li-ttle birds in sweet re-frain,
> Sing all day long, a me-rry song,
> The ha-ppy birds with ne'er a care,
> In sweet re-frain be-yond com-pare.

She could hardly miss the way even this simple song was laced with lascivious intent.

DURING ALL THIS TIME Karolina dreamt persistently, night after night. As if a theme had been introduced that was being developed nightly in various ways. All the men she had known appeared in her dreams: lovers, adversaries, friends. She dreamt as if she were turning over stones to see who might be lurking under them—a frog, a prince, a man who held the key. The man who would restore her to a state of sleepy innocence; who would love her always. As if each night she would round up everyone she had ever known or loved, abused or scorned or hated, in order that they may appear before her once again and she may thoroughly reassess and reconsider every possibility.

And on their daily excursions into the veld, with nothing in sight but stones and parched, tufted grass, her thoughts strayed increasingly to the women she knew, to all the women she had ever known—to every single woman she had considered a friend. She weighed up each one in turn. Who might be the one who would never let her down? Basil pointed out all sorts of things to her, she did not take in anything he said—she gazed into his untroubled eyes as if she expected the image of a woman to take shape in his unblemished irises.

She had come to this place to research the survival strategies of a species of moth of the *Geometridae* family. On the way she had given a lift to Basil, a complete stranger. She had entered a caravan—against the backdrop of a bloody sunset over the undulating hills of the Natal midlands—and she had had her lightly perspiring palm read by a woman crowned with a nest of gilded hair. This woman had said some absurd, unsubstantiated things. Karolina had laughed as she emerged from the caravan at the presumption of it all. (She happened to be a scientist, her entomological research was widely respected.) But no matter how derisive her laughter, the woman's words continued to haunt her.

On Wednesday evening before dinner Karolina and Basil went out on the front stoep for a drink, to find once more, as on the day of their first arrival, Jess Jankowitz and his friend. Jess rose from his chair, Karolina introduced him to Basil; Jess introduced his friend

Frans Roeg. They remarked on the weather; Karolina and Basil took a separate table a short distance away.

It was a lovely night. After the fierce heat of the day, the cool of dusk settled intimately on their skins. Her dark hair was badly cut, but tonight her shoulders curved softly. Having mended her former foolish ways, Karolina had resolved long ago to keep a low emotional profile. She led an exemplary life—devoting her energies to the study of moths. Even at the tender age of twelve, before she had lost everything, her knowledge of entomology had been impressive.

Karolina and Basil rose to go to dinner. She said goodbye to Jess over her shoulder. There was a goodbye from Frans too, accompanied by a pained half-smile and an unfathomable, lingering look. Does he still have his money on the red one? she asked Basil in the dining room. Once again he merely laughed—she should be more patient, he said.

On Thursday afternoon she went to the Rendezvous Café for a cup of tea. She found Jess there. As she entered, he half rose from his chair, drew out one for her. She sat down at his table. He ordered a fresh pot, for two. Together they drank the undrinkable tea. The ceiling fan turned steadily above their heads. It was again the wearisome hour of the scarab. The main street, the side streets, the surrounding veld lay inert in the murderous summer heat. In the front section of the café overripe mangos and wilted grapes were displayed in straw boxes. The heavy, sweet smell of mangos filled the entire room. Jess wiped the sweat from his face with a handkerchief.

On the table before him lay the book with the red cover, the guide to a clear mind.

Has he mastered the techniques set out in it? she asked.

"No," he said, "but I seem to have more peace of mind." He had an unusual voice. Somewhat hesitant, and not very deep for someone his size.

He told her that this practice had been giving his life focus and meaning for some time now.

What had he been interested in before? she asked.

"Oh, before," he said, "before, I aspired to worldly success; I desired women, often to no avail. All my life I'd waited for a breakthrough, something that would reveal my true, inalienable superiority."

"And did that ever happen?" she asked.

"No," he said, "it never did."

"And the women?" she asked, after some brief hesitation.

"The women didn't amount to much either," he said. "They brought little lasting joy."

"Is there someone now?" she asked. She noticed that the two of them were reflected in the mirror on the rear wall.

"There was until recently," he replied after a brief pause.

Karolina nodded wordlessly. The smell of mangos was overpoweringly sweet and heavy. She finished her tea.

"Will you come out for a walk with me this evening?" he asked. "The evenings are beautiful, and it's not so hot then."

Karolina thought it over briefly. "All right," she said.

She rose and said goodbye. As she emerged from the café, she was hit by a wave of heat. She seemed to be the only living creature out on the street. Lieutenant Kieliemann was watching her from behind a pillar on the other side of the street, eating peanuts and raisins from a small packet, but this she did not know.

High up in the cloudless sky the moon was visible, so pale as to be almost translucent.

After dinner she met Jess on the front stoep of the hotel. They walked along Stiebeuel Street. The moon gradually began to take on more substance. It reminded him of a Chinese film he once saw, Jess said. What was so memorable about this film? she asked.

"One was relentlessly confronted with death, like in few other films," he replied, "but also with a dreadful inevitability, with a devastating sense of just how terrible things can be."

They turned left into Johanna Brand Street, accompanied by the moon. The sky had opened up like the pupil of an eye.

She told him she had a passion for cypress trees. They walked along the wide pavements, past the large, old-fashioned homes. They all looked vaguely familiar, but she couldn't recognise a single one, too much time had gone by.

She did not tell him of her own relentless preoccupation with death and mortality. She did not tell him of her passion for dancing. She did not ask about Frans Roeg, though she was keen to find out more about him.

Jess asked about Basil. She told him that she had given him a lift on her way here; that they had never met before. She told Jess that they spent their mornings working together in the veld, that Basil lodged with a Mr. Quiroga, with whom he continued his study of natural remedies. Meeting Basil like that seemed to her preordained, although this was not the kind of language she normally used.

This was the mood of their conversation as they walked the wide streets of the town, under the radiant moon. They went as far as the western boundary, right up to the wire fence where the veld began, before they turned back to the hotel.

He asked if they could meet again.

ON FRIDAY NIGHT Basil and Karolina went to play snooker.

On their way they stopped at the ladies' bar for a drink. The magistrate, she saw, was ensconced in his usual corner. She decided she had no great desire to be seen or to be addressed by him. Pol had not arrived yet.

Inside the snooker room things were heating up. Kieliemann looked up briefly when Karolina and Basil entered, Sergeant Frikkie Visser smiled broadly. Apart from Sergeants Yap Buytendach and Boet Visagie, and the two teachers Kriek and Botha, yet another teacher had joined the ranks tonight—a certain Baluschagne (wood-work and rugby), called Balls by everyone there—a shortish, attractive fellow with well-developed pectorals and a devastating smile, unmistakably a ladies' man. In addition there were a few salesmen (in transit), and one of the local doctors, a Doctor Manie Maritz, with a pronounced limp and a lecherous eye. Also, three farmers from the surrounding area—among them the two De Melck brothers, the owners of a large stud farm in the district (extremely wealthy in spite of the drought, as she was to find out later). The younger brother was golden blond, radiantly blond—compellingly blond—and tended to keep to himself even while surrounded by others, she observed.

Do the women ever come to play snooker? Karolina asked Basil while they were taking a break from the game. Oh yes, said Basil, once the ants started flying, the women would come. At that moment Pol put his head round the door. His saw Karolina and waved at her, glass in hand, his head tilted endearingly.

Karolina played recklessly tonight. She drank a great deal of whisky. When it was her turn to shoot, her shoulders gleamed beneath the heavy light over the snooker table. Her hair had taken on a life of its own. As the evening wore on, the air grew thick with smoke, with the excitement of the game, with disjointed talk, with laughter, with the heat generated by the bodies of those present. Outside the wide-open windows the night was cool and blue. The warm light drew insects—they came in large numbers, insisted on coming in, on being identified.

From the ladies' bar next door, fragments of song wafted towards them, interspersed with regular bursts of laughter at an ever-rising pitch. The laughter was coming from the magistrate in his corner, Karolina realised eventually.

Kieliemann was watching her like a hawk, though unobtrusively. Whenever she leaned over to play a shot, he moved in behind her so as to rub the blue Terylene bulge against her buttocks. Doctor Maritz, too, undeterred by his limp, went to great lengths to establish some sort of physical contact, but he was less agile than Kieliemann.

Karolina's game grew increasingly reckless; her head was spinning; the green surface of the table, the whisky, the heat, all combined to induce a hallucinatory state. A menacing yellow glow bounced off the walls, there was incessant talk. The De Melck brothers drank brandy and discussed Hereford bloodlines. They talked of sperm counts and testicles. The three teachers talked of rugby. Two bright red patches appeared on the cheeks of the most lustreless of the three (Mr. Kriek). The psyches were slowly unravelling. The atmosphere grew dense with inarticulate longing, with concealed fear and prejudice, with latent hysteria rising gradually to the surface. It was bound to break through tonight—a raid would perhaps be organised, or a midnight pillaging party. In a corner of the room Balls announced that his cock was taking on alarming proportions (Karolina heard in passing), and from the adjoining room waves of Pol's singing and the magistrate's laughter rose relentlessly.

When exactly were they supposed to go out tonight? Karolina heard Sergeant Frikkie ask Kieliemann immediately after he had played his shot. She strained to hear, but failed to pick up more than this.

Shortly afterwards she went to the toilet (as unobtrusively as possible) by way of the back door. Kieliemann was waiting in the corridor she had to cross on the way back.

As on the previous occasion, he pressed her up against the wall. This time he had had more to drink, and there was a greater urgency to his pleading: "Please," he begged, "don't refuse me."

"Will you damn well leave me alone!" she said, and pushed him away violently. But as she was about to open the door leading into the snooker room, she turned and asked: "Where do you plan to go tonight?"

He paused, giving her a brief, strange look. "Why, do you want to come along?" he asked.

"Yes," she replied on a sudden impulse.

"There's big shit in the location," he said. "Come along by all means, if you really want to see."

Karolina went into the snooker room, Kieliemann following close behind.

On the other side of the menacing green surface of the snooker table stood Captain Gert Els. He had probably come in while Kieliemann was forcing his attentions on her in the corridor off the snooker room. His hair and skin were devoid of colour, his eyes pale and expressionless, the lower lids red-rimmed. He seemed to be sweating profusely.

"His mother's cunt," he said emphatically, tapping rhythmically with his baton against his thigh.

Els summoned Kieliemann to his side with a mere jerk of the head. They conferred briefly. Sergeants Frikkie, Yap, and Boet were rounded up in the same way, and the entire gang departed; Kieliemann without as much as a backward glance at Karolina.

"I can't breathe in here," she told Basil. "I'm going outside." On the cool stoep she said: "Kieliemann says there's some sort of trouble in the township—they must be on their way there right now."

"If there is trouble, you can be sure they're the ones who have caused it," said Basil, and spat out something he had been chewing on with some vehemence. "It's past midnight," he said, "the hour of the rat."

"What does that mean?" she asked.

"Els and the rat are a bad combination," Basil replied. "Two rats make a pack."

Basil wished her a peaceful night. (Karolina felt a certain reluctance at the parting, an unwillingness to let him go; she had need of reassurance.)

She went up the stairs, keeping one hand on the wooden handrail. She walked down the passage with its worn carpet to her room. (She had to start looking for other lodgings.)

For a while she remained seated on her bed in the dark. Her head reeled; she had had too much whisky. Through the open window the night sky was visible. It was bright and clear. The moon was small and high up in the sky. The hotel had by no means settled down for the night. Doors slammed, toilets flushed, footsteps and laughter sounded down the corridor. Floorboards creaked. A woman's low voice was audible in the adjoining room. Perhaps it was the lovers. Somewhere, far away, down below, there was a great commotion.

The room was filled with moths, a rich variety of shapes and sizes; some of these she would have expected to find here, but not all. Before she got into bed, she checked them, as she always did, to determine the various genera and species.

What was the beautiful woman's story, she wondered before she fell asleep. Would she be blinded, consumed and ultimately destroyed by love?

31

Karolina slept fitfully. Once she was woken by a yellow light flashing in the street outside the hotel, a police light. What are they doing here? she thought drowsily.

She dreamt she was going down on some man, she practically fell forward on his penis, she took him in her mouth, but time and again he was unable to sustain an erection. The man was Jess.

On her way to town the next morning she saw that posters announcing a prayer meeting for rain to be held at the local flying club had been added to the posters advertising the play *The Jealous Husband*.

It was Saturday, she would be going to the dance tonight. But this time the prospect failed to provide the customary, pleasurable sense of anticipation. She tried to recall where the town prison was situated. It seemed unlikely she had ever known its whereabouts. Twenty-five years ago, the municipal swimming baths, the Oasis and the Rendezvous Cafés, Nortjé's Chemist, the town hall where films were shown, the Avbob Funeral Parlour, the veld that bordered the far side of the town, and the flying club located along its right-hand boundary had been the main landmarks here, as far as she had been concerned.

TONIGHT KAROLINA danced once more with the Kolyn fellow in the hotel dining room. He was dressed in short trousers because of the heat, and he wore trendy white American sneakers that laced up to the ankle. He had large, shapely calves; delicately jointed ankles, knees and wrists; a sturdy stomach and buttocks. An early eruption of acne had left his skin scarred and pitted. These scars were now camouflaged by a neatly trimmed, though lush Voortrekker beard, which did not leave much of his mouth visible. His large, dark-brown eyes were wide-set. His nose seemed at odds with his face—too fine and narrow in that bearded landscape. Legs, head, and torso somehow failed to form a harmonious whole. He held her lightly by the right hand, nevertheless managing to sweep her round the floor at a terrific pace. He was an accomplished dancer, but his movements were mechanical, like those of a person who had been taught to dance in the army.

Karolina danced without inspiration. Between dances they drank orange squash on the stoep beneath the multicoloured lights. Over his shoulder she stared at the moon distractedly. He spoke about Hereford stud cattle, agricultural relief aid schemes, seamless irrigation dams. Drought and drought talk, all kinds of bullshit that she hardly listened to, nor believed a word of. It seemed he was some sort of government official, or government representative, she couldn't care less right then.

Round and round they whirled. With mighty strides he swept her round the floor, until it seemed the muscles of her inner thighs would tear with the strain of keeping up. He was dripping with perspiration. She experienced a certain displaced pleasure at the touch of his sturdy, sweaty stomach.

In the background there was a great din from the snooker room; there was raucous singing in the ladies' bar—one end of which opened into the dining room.

At eleven o'clock she excused herself and went up the carved baroque stairway to her room.

She no longer expected immediate gratification. The study of moths and the refinement of her dance technique, these were the objects of her passion. She expected nothing at all from any man, woman, or lover—whatever the predictions of the woman with the gilded nest. To avoid conflict and shame, unnecessary pain, emotional disruption, coming to a violent end, this was her firm resolve. She was perfectly content. A hundred times better off than before.

Next time she would go dancing in a neighbouring town by herself.

ON SUNDAY she lay on her bed, shutting out the world outside. She ate nothing, she drank only water. She was not happy and she was not unhappy. She slept and she woke up. The mother appeared in her dreams, taking on many different forms. She was good, she was bad, she was nurturing, she was rejecting. The mother was young, she was old, she was pregnant, she was dead; and time and again, as Karolina woke from this half-sleep, as the world took on solid substance once more, she would realise that the mother was no longer there for her. It caused her grief.

The landscapes that came to her! The guises taken on by the father! Her own sexuality, masked in so many ways! And the friends, the acquaintances, the loved and the dead ones who put in an appearance, who merged with one another, who came up with suggestions, who traded in mysteries! The Technicolor close-ups, the guest appearances, the inexplicable debuts and gestures, the grimaces, the threats! The intimate crowd that rose up to meet Karolina, that embraced her and held her close, that coerced her, confided in her, cherished, taunted, abandoned her!

Towards the end of the afternoon she rose and went to the window. She gazed out over the sleeping town, drained of all colour by the dry, late-summer heat. A moth perched on the windowsill. It was a rare species: *Chrysophasma vrystatensis*. It was small and blond, the wings coming together in an acute triangle, rooted at the apex, quite close to the head. The head was miniscule; the wings were stiff, like gold brocade delicately embroidered with silver thread.

Anything might happen, Karolina thought. She might experience anything, be exposed to anything; she had no claim on any sort of security—ultimately there was none. There were no guarantees.

CHAPTER 3

"**FOR ANY TYPE** of trauma, mental or physical, even if it was incurred a long time ago," said Basil. "For disorders of the blood, for festering conditions, black-and-blue spots, or a tendency to bleed. To prevent the formation of pus. For evil-smelling secretions. If the muscles are tender and feel bruised. For abscesses that fail to ripen. For the harmful effect of trauma, financial loss, rage, and revenge; for impotence brought on by excessive sexual activity. If a person fears illness, or sudden death, or great crowds, or public places."

He lifted a small herb from the soil.

"If there is a compelling urge to pick at the scalp, or at the bed, or at the wall. If the head feels hot and the body cold. If the right eye seems larger than the left, if blood oozes from the ears. If there is a sensitivity to high-pitched sounds."

Karolina squatted next to Basil. He held up the herb for her to see.

"If the skin looks dark and spotty, and the smallest abrasion turns into a bruise. If the person dreams of death and of mutilated bodies, wakes up in a state of terror—all these things indicate the use of the remedy prepared from this herb," he said.

Karolina studied the herb attentively. She did not know if Basil was making fun of her. He seemed perfectly serious.

"Look closely at the shape of the leaves, they're spiky and pointed, and the flower is blue with a black centre," he said.

"How do you remember it all?" asked Karolina.

"Once you have a clear overall picture of the disorder," Basil said, "it's not difficult to remember the detail." He held the little plant in his hand, both of them still looking at it." How do you manage to remember all the insects, all the families and orders and all?" he asked.

"I've never had any difficulty with that," said Karolina, "I've had an interest in it ever since I was a child. My father began to teach me when I was very young."

She fell silent. There was no sound other than the murderous shrilling of the cicadas (order *Hemiptera*, family *Cicadidae*).

"One might say I learnt it at my father's knee," she said after a while. "He was an entomologist too."

She squatted next to Basil, who was easing the little plant into a brown paper bag.

"I disappointed him," she said. "And he disappointed me." She watched the ceaseless activity of ants at her feet. They were large and black.

"He died before I had achieved anything," she said.

Basil looked at her keenly for a moment, as if making a marginal adjustment to his general assessment of her.

"At the time of his death we no longer had much contact. I was told he suffered a great deal towards the end." She scratched aimlessly in the sand with a small twig. "He did not have an easy death."

She continued to scratch in the sand. "Something like your remedies might have helped him, perhaps. To let go, you know," she opened her hand, "to let go of life."

Basil stuck a label on the brown paper bag. He said nothing.

"So you see what comes of having an interest from an early age," he said after a while.

Karolina noticed that Basil's speech seemed more formal sometimes, and at other times less so. (Was there a touch of irony directed at himself in his periodic use of a more regional Afrikaans?) She did not know him well enough to understand or predict his speech variations.

"Look," he said, pointing at a large, hairy spider in a web. It was female, a two-lunged *Labidognatha* species, Karolina saw.

"You can cure many things with the remedy extracted from the venom of this spider," said Basil. "It acts upon the heart, the spine, the respiratory system. The symptoms appear suddenly and they're fairly violent." He gave a small laugh. "It counteracts the harmful effect of unrequited love. It relieves the suffering of those in the throes of death—and of those driven mad by lust."

Karolina observed the spider as it rocked in its web. When she was very young, spiders, too, in their great variety, had held an endless fascination for her. So many guises! So many schemes!

She kept an unobtrusive watch on Basil while they were at work. He had a well-proportioned head, and his mind was ordered too, she thought. A clear head. His movements were quiet; he did not say much, he spoke unemphatically, as if reluctant to draw attention to himself. What had made her stop to pick him up? She did not know; she never gave lifts.

They spent the entire morning moving slowly through the veld. Karolina jotted down her own observations; looked at the things Basil pointed out to her. It was hot. The veld abounded with stones and plants: she had never been aware of them in quite the same way before.

The remedies are prepared from a range of vegetable, animal, or mineral substances, Basil explained. But these raw materials are continuously refined so as to become practically indiscernible, until finally hardly a single molecule of the original substance remained. Mr. Quiroga prepared new remedies all the time; Basil acted as his assistant. Mr. Quiroga came here from Argentina ten years ago. He had a vast knowledge of the subject, said Basil. There were few to equal him in this country.

"Where did you grow up, Basil?" Karolina asked.

"On the Cape Flats," he said.

"Is there an abundance of plants there?" she asked.

"Not in the area where I grew up," he replied. "But there is an abundance of needy and traumatised people."

They sat under the willow tree by the dry spruit. They ate egg sandwiches, which they bought at the Springbok Café every morning. They drank water from a bottle, or tea from a Thermos. It was the hottest time of day.

"What will you do with that root you collected," Karolina asked, "the root that looks like a finger?"

"That's a potent one," said Basil, "that one's a deep remedy. If we can get it right, it can cure deep psychotic conditions. Deep delusions. But it's tricky—you have to know how to use it, or it can do a lot of harm. Call up very angry things."

IN THE AFTERNOON Karolina and Basil drove to a neighbouring town, somewhat larger than Voorspoed, to pick up a parcel for Mr. Quiroga, whose car had broken down. This may be pure coincidence, or it may be preordained, Karolina thought—she had stopped to give a lift to this stranger, and now she was travelling with him along a road she might never have taken if she had been on her own. How extraordinary.

Along the way they came upon the scene of an accident. They saw a stationary car and a pick-up truck on the same side of the road, a few hundred metres apart. Basil indicated that she should pull over. He jumped out and Karolina followed close behind. (If she had been on her own she would have driven by, she would have gone for help.)

The driver of the car lay sprawled to one side, flung clear of his vehicle and halfway down the embankment. The driver of the pick-up truck was slumped forward in his seat. Blood had oozed from his ears and his nose and had dried in thin streaks across his face. His head resembled an urn that had been shattered and patched together again, leaving fine, visible cracks. His eyes were swollen shut, as if he had been crying over something for a long time. He sat motionless, solitary, attentive.

Karolina took in all of this in an instant, in the few moments it took to get to the pick-up truck and to run back to the man on the ground. He was lying on his stomach. The earth beneath him was soaked. Basil turned him over carefully. He wore short trousers; a jet of blood spurted freely, like a fountain, from a deep gash in his leg. Basil remarked on the colour of the blood. Bright red, because it was pumping away so fast, he said. The man appeared to be unconscious, but his eyes were half open; he was whimpering. Basil took off his shirt, tore it into strips, tied them tightly round the wound. He took two small phials from a small leather pouch he was carrying. He got Karolina to hold the man's head, tilting the neck back slightly. Carefully he shook a few tiny tablets into the mouth, under the tongue.

"This will stop the heavy bleeding and prevent shock," said Basil.

He examined the man briefly. (A young man.) Found no serious injury. Feel here, he said to Karolina, one hand is burning hot, the other icy cold. The man's body was quite rigid, his arms and legs jerked at regular intervals. They should move him to the car very carefully, said Basil, showing her where to take hold of him. It was very hot, they sweated profusely, sweat ran into Karolina's eyes. They carried the injured man up the steep embankment, moving forward one step at a time; getting him onto the back seat required considerable effort.

Karolina took a last look at the attentive corpse in the pick-up truck. She drove fast; Basil kept a constant watch on the injured man, placing more of the tiny pills under his tongue at regular intervals.

"The guy in the pick-up truck died some time ago," he said, "long before this man was injured."

"What does that mean?" asked Karolina.

"It means it was a very unusual accident," said Basil.

On reaching the town, they dropped the injured man off at the hospital first and reported the accident to the police afterwards.

Only then did they get round to picking up Mr. Quiroga's parcel at a sturdy stone house in Rooibult Street, next door to the Majuba Trading Store. It was almost five o'clock, the streets were crowded, the heat was stifling. Surely that mountain can't be too far from here, said Basil as he got out of the car—Majuba, where the Boers and the English fought their battle. Karolina waited for him in the car, scanned the horizon unenthusiastically, saw no mountain. Right now she couldn't care less what the Boers and the English had been up to in these parts. Her mouth was dry. People hung about noisily outside the Majuba Trading Store, waiting for taxis and lifts.

When Basil returned with the parcel, he suggested that they should find a place to have tea. Karolina accepted gratefully.

She bent her head over her tea.

Basil sat quietly facing her.

"I've been content up to now," she said at last. "I was perfectly content until recently. I could keep everything at a distance. But now, all of a sudden I can no longer do so. I feel caught up in everything. And detached from everything too. So detached, and so caught up. A strange feeling." She spoke more urgently. "I don't know what I've done with my life! I don't know if I can still love someone!" (She started, why speak of love all of a sudden?) "I can't open my hand," she said, opening her hand, her palm facing upward, "I can't let go."

She broke off suddenly, resting her elbow on the table, covering her mouth with her hand.

"I think of death all the time," she said. "Whenever I'm not thinking of the moths."

Two men entered the café as she spoke, but Karolina was too upset to notice them immediately.

"Do you dream of great masses of water?" asked Basil.

"Yes," said Karolina.

"Do you dream of insects?"

"Yes," she said.

"Do you cross unfamiliar landscapes in your dreams?"

"Yes," she said.

"What else?" asked Basil.

"Everyone I've ever known seems to be turning up in my dreams lately," said Karolina. "No matter if they're dead or alive."

Basil took a small phial from the leather pouch.

"Take this," he said. "Put it on your tongue."

Karolina stretched her neck forward, tilted her head back (as she had done with the injured man that morning) and received the tiny, sweetish pills on her tongue like a sacramental wafer.

From the corner of her eye she saw that both men were looking directly at them now.

"Good heavens, Basil!" she whispered when the men resumed their conversation. "It's the lover! It's the man we saw at the cemetery the other day!"

The next time they saw him would be on stage, at the performance of *The Jealous Husband* the following Saturday night.

KAROLINA WENT for another walk with Jess two days after the accident. As on the previous occasion, they walked up Stiebeuel Street. She remembered the dream he had appeared in some nights ago.

Initially she felt uncommunicative, and they walked in silence. She had been feeling depressed and anxious ever since the accident. She had never known that blood could spurt so brightly, and the attentive corpse remained with her. It was a strange accident, Basil had said. Was it possible that one accident covered up another? She had worked on her own yesterday and this morning, she had not seen Basil. On their way back to town she had been struck again by the severity of the drought in the region. The pans and dams were empty, the exposed mud sediment cracked and dry. The maize burnt to the ground or withered away. A spirit of disquiet, of discontent throughout the land, like Karolina's own mood tonight.

But the night was beautiful, she saw. The firmament, at least, had not yet withered away—the night sky was rich and velvety, densely strewn with stars. The moon was small and sleek, like something that had lain underwater for a long time. Moist, like the smooth white ball of an eye.

The man walked next to her. She was aware of the intensity of his skin, of the glow he emitted even in the dark. She did not know anyone with a similar complexion. She had never known a man before with as warm, as ruddy and freckled a bodily surface. No wonder he was drawn to a book with a flaming cover. It must seem like a mirror to him, reflecting his own glow.

"Tell me more about the path to a clear mind," she said.

"Suffering and false perceptions are caused by an attachment to things," Jess said. "Everything one clings to unduly becomes an obstacle."

"Can one escape this?" she asked. "Escape the suffering?"

"One can," he said. He spoke softly, haltingly. "One can understand suffering by understanding the true nature of reality. And by cultivating a greater awareness of the present moment."

They walked up Andries Pretorius Street in silence.

"Do you find it painful," she asked after a while, "the breakdown of your last relationship?"

"Yes, I do," he replied. "I had hoped for a long time that it would work."

"Does meditation help you deal with the pain?" she asked.

"Yes, it does," he replied.

When they reached the wire fence that separated the town from the veld, they turned back.

"And you?" he asked. "Is there someone in your life?"

"No," she replied. "There's no one."

He did not pursue the matter.

"Will you come away with me this weekend?" he asked unexpectedly. "I'll be staying in Wakkerspruit for a few days, at a house belonging to an aunt of my friend Frans Roeg's."

Karolina declined quite bluntly, without a moment's hesitation.

When she was back in her room again, she studied herself in the mirror. Her hair was dark, it was badly cut. It seemed inert—like a potted palm.

As she lay in her bed, before going to sleep, she studied her palm by the light of the moon: her hand was hot and dry now.

Why did she turn down this man's invitation, and the promise of warmth it held?

Because she could no longer imagine a different sort of life.

THE PERFORMANCE on Saturday night was an extraordinary event. It was the story of a man driven by jealousy to murder his innocent wife. He is deceived by his best friend. He is led to believe that his wife has been unfaithful to him. It was obvious which 'classic hit' this play was based on. And besides, the husband's skin was artificially darkened. It was hard to tell what the audience made of it.

Everybody was there. People crowded round the cake tables in the foyer during the interval. Pol was there, waving at Karolina with a can of Coke (dash of Coke, generous measure of brandy) in one hand and a koeksister in the other; his face dripping with perspiration, his smile wide, oily and impenetrable. The FAK individuals were there, wearing handknit pullovers, accompanied by their girlfriends. The De Melck brothers were there, accompanied by wives in expensive outfits. (The younger brother looked unhappy.) Karolina caught Kieliemann's lecherous eye in passing. A small number of black inhabitants from the township were there—they stood to one side and at a safe distance; they sat in the back rows. The beautiful woman was there, Karolina noted with interest.

After the interval everyone filed back meekly into the hall, Karolina was somewhat surprised that it had not run empty. The jealous (blackened) husband's presence was even more compelling in the second act. He was played by the lover. His name was Jurie Beyers, it said in the programme. The beautiful woman sat in the third row from the front with her husband and two small children, who slumped sleepily against her. She listened with rapt attention; she seemed spellbound, her profile motionless in the dark. Manie Delarey, the man who had been in the café with Beyers a couple of days before, played the father of the unhappy bride—there was a fair amount of forcefulness, brutality and sensuality to his rendering of the part. The bride was tense and fragile, almost unbearably trusting; all artless surrender—to the point of recklessness, just about. A trembling moth. All the characters fell victim to their own best intentions, to a corrupt, exploitative regime. The play was set somewhere in post-colonial Africa. The father was a high-ranking, powerful government official, the son-in-law an honourable military man—he was dark (very dark), appreciably darker than his radiant, white bride. (Jurie Beyers, artificially darkened so as to drive home the contrast.) The villainous friend was a white, military colleague—deceitful, cunning, sexy; inscrutable, ruthless, politically ambitious; oedipally obsessed and anally fixated. He was played by a woman.

"What do we have here?" Karolina whispered to Basil in the dark.

The audience sat riveted to their seats throughout. The dialogue was in a dense, insinuating Afrikaans. Some of the phrases had a strangely familiar ring to them—he would rather be a frog, the tormented husband said, living on the poisonous vapours of a cellar, than surrender the smallest part of the person he loved for someone else's use. The final scene was a miracle of lighting and dramatic intensity. It looked as if cold, blue moonlight were falling through the ornate grid of a window and onto the marital bed, where the gruesome deed was done. ("First I kissed her, then I killed her!") (Every hair on Karolina's body stood on end.) When the husband realised that he had been cruelly deceived by his friend, he shot himself. Tell them, were his dying words, that in my own way I have served the state honourably—they know that—and that I have destroyed my most precious possession! Dramatic stuff—political aspirations, betrayal, murder, suicide. The audience left the hall dejectedly. Outside, the night sky was high, the stars bright.

"What did Beyers and Delarey hope to achieve by putting on this play?" Karolina asked Basil as he walked her back to the hotel. "Because there does seem to be something decidedly odd about this production," she said.

"Jurie Beyers was very active in the struggle on the Cape Flats in 1985 and '86," said Basil.

"Do you know him then?" asked Karolina.

"We've met," said Basil.

"And the other man? Delarey?" she asked.

"That man knows how to persuade people," Basil replied.

"Why didn't you tell me the other day?" she asked.

"You didn't want to know then," said Basil.

KAROLINA FERREIRA was walking from the café to the hotel on Sunday morning when a blue police vehicle pulled up next to her with screeching brakes. Lieutenant Kieliemann stuck his head out of the window; he asked if Karolina still wanted to come along to the location. (Not township he called it, but location.) She hesitated briefly, then got into the back of the car next to Sergeant Boet Visagie. A policeman she had not seen before was in the front seat next to Kieliemann.

"Lieutenant Worcester," he mumbled over his shoulder. (Not talkative today.)

"Has something happened?" she asked Visagie in a low voice.

"Big shit," he replied.

They sped along the dirt road, enveloped in a cloud of dust. Karolina saw nothing much through the window. She had never been here before. How long had this township been in existence? There was not much talk. The men in the back and the front of the car were all bristling whiskers and grim determination; the raised adrenalin levels were palpable. She felt her own mouth go dry, her heartbeat accelerate. She looked fixedly over her left shoulder at the miserable, dry veld. It was cloudy, but there was no hope of rain.

The township seemed to be composed of all the places one would never voluntarily choose to go. Neither the few solitary trees nor the surrounding low hills redeemed the bleakness of the scene. (Did it seem this way because she was an outsider? Karolina wondered.) They drove to a spot where little groups of people were gathered in the street outside a small shack.

They got out. A second police vehicle was already on the scene. By now the dust had settled. The chaos and confusion that had led up to these events had died down. Karolina saw the dead lying under blankets in the back of the police van. The last of these was being lifted onto a stretcher. Rigor mortis had already set in. He was lifted by the hands and feet, since he no longer needed to be supported at the waist. The bystanders looked on. Karolina tried to remain as inconspicuous as possible, she could not read the expressions on their faces. Children snivelled and clung to their mothers' skirts.

Kieliemann was asking questions. His muscles bulging with resentment and with a repressed urge to engage in cleansing action. The more slightly built, richly whiskered Lieutenant Worcester, who stood next to him, was equally tense and ready to go. But everyone's attention soon shifted to the next scene.

People were beginning to gather excitedly outside a neighbouring house, where it looked as if the bystanders were trying to restrain someone, trying to prevent him from entering.

Gert Els came out of this house, followed by two black constables. He was pale, with large sweat marks under the arms, and he was tapping his baton against his thigh. He looked grim, irritable, at the end of his patience. He paused momentarily, scraping clean the heel of his boot on the cement steps. (Like Mrs. Macbeth?) Karolina retreated behind a small group of bystanders.

Only after Els and the two constables had left the house, the man who was being held back was released. There were a few moments of silence—nothing but this man and his breathless terror. Then he ran into the house.

Karolina did not know how much time it took. She did not know what the man was confronted with inside his home. This one behind an upturned bedstead, that one by the cupboard. His home churned up as if by a herd of swine. His wife, his child, a second child, other family members: stabbed, hacked to pieces, dishonoured.

The sun broke through the clouds.

After some time the man came out. He stood there facing the small, silent crowd. What could he say? What possible public expression could he give to his horror? After the subdued light inside, his face was screwed up against the bright sunlight.

He looked as though he had had some sort of revelation in there, Karolina thought. He looked as if he might want to say: I myself have come face to face with God! I am acquainted with his awful plan!

The crowd parted silently, clearing a path for him. He staggered past them.

Karolina gazed after him. He looked as if he had been branded, she thought. It seemed as if whatever he had seen had been burnt into the retinas of his eyes.

A few yards away he was stopped by a photographer, who wanted to take some photographs. (Where had he come from all of a sudden?)

When the man had passed them, the crowd descended on the house. They had to see for themselves. They had to see the dead, had to see how death had been anticipated, resisted, and ultimately embraced. The police did not restrain them.

Gert Els and the constables drove off immediately in the yellow police van (with its load of dead in the back). They disappeared in an aggressive column of dust.

Karolina walked back to the remaining police vehicle.

"They can clean up the mess themselves," Visagie said.

"Let the dead bury their own dead," Kieliemann said.

"Why were only some of the dead taken away?" Karolina asked.

"The people say they are from another place. Their families will have to come and claim their bodies in town," Kieliemann said, "we don't want any more shit."

They drove back to town in silence.

Karolina huddled deep into the back seat. She wanted to remove herself physically from the presence of these men. What was she but an innocent, an idiot? A shameful thing to be, she thought. She had no understanding of the whole, or of the way in which all these terrible and implacable elements fitted together.

CHAPTER 4

AFTER THE EVENTS of the weekend Karolina avoided the men in the snooker room. She did not want to see them or be seen by them. Gert Els in particular she wanted to avoid. They could blunder along in whatever destructive way they chose. She would stay out of their way.

The image of the man who had staggered out of his house in the township haunted her. She could not forget his face.

Together she and Basil moved deeper into the veld. She would at times become light-headed with the heat and with the intense effort required by her search for the occurrence and distribution of the species *Hebdomophruda crenilinea*. Basil's smooth brown skin darkened gradually. Karolina's complexion took on a deeper tone, she lost her unhealthy pallor.

As they moved through the veld, he would point out something here, something there, similarities, differences; a plant here, a leaf there, a flower; seeds, roots, thorns, insects, stones, trees. He specified the properties of the remedies obtained from all these various raw components. Each remedy presents a coherent picture, can be seen as a constellation of symptoms—no single symptom exists in isolation. Basil pointed out the general effect of each of the various remedies as well as its specific effect on the eyes, the ears, the nose, the mouth, the throat, the stomach, the urinary system, the reproductive organs, the respiratory system, the heart, the neck and back, the limbs, the skin. The effects on a person's sleep cycles and on his psyche. She was particularly interested in these references to disorders of the psyche—anxiety, fear, and conflict; guilt feelings and delusions; despair, destructiveness and withdrawal.

The human body with its organs and systems now seemed to Karolina to be like an enormous map—to which additional information may constantly be added.

Because she had hitherto devoted herself to the study of insects, she tended to see the human species (order *Primate,* family *Hominidae*) as no more than a subdivision in the broad order of the animal kingdom. A subdivision of the subphylum *Vertebrata*—of no more importance than the other subphylum *Invertebrata,* the subject of her research. (Its principal focus being the phylum *Arthropoda,* class *Insecta,* with its twenty-nine orders.)

Here in the veld with Basil she saw that man was a vast territory. Basil opened up a whole new world to her. She grew so absorbed and fascinated that at times she almost lost sight of her own search, and at times even resented the claims this new way of seeing made on her.

Basil was a good teacher. His mind, she saw, was as remarkably well organised as his head—which was strikingly harmonious in its proportions—and as perfectly balanced.

EVERY AFTERNOON, when the town and the hotel were dead quiet, when the entire landscape lay inert in the murderous summer heat, Karolina would lie on her bed on the stiff, cool sheets, contemplating all she had recently seen and heard. She would turn these things over in her mind. She would observe them, she would weigh them as if on a small hand scale; she would allow everything to lie, to ripen, to stir, to sink, to rise up to the surface, to sink once more, and sometimes to disappear from sight. She felt as if her mind were being churned up daily, causing the contents at the bottom to rise, so that everything was set in motion and turned cloudy, opaque. Old things, old contents surfaced, things she had not given a thought for many years.

One afternoon she thought, so, Gert Els, you fucker, you bastard—you and the other one, the magistrate. The one who pisses a forked stream. You and your vicious predecessors—replicas, all. Birds of a feather. Episodes that are better not mentioned, better forgotten. Unpleasant remains—part of the murky sediment.

JESS RANG, asked if she would like to come for a walk that evening. They met outside the hotel. She asked what his weekend had been like. Pleasant, he said, and asked about hers. She gave a brief account of the performance, but said nothing just then, of her visit to the township.

He asked if she had seen the sunset that evening, it had been quite spectacular. Yes, she said—it had been unusually dramatic. But the drought seemed quite severe, had he, too, seen signs of it along the way?

He replied in the affirmative. They walked on in silence. Tonight they walked a different route, down Marthinus Wessels Street, which led towards the cemetery. The sky seemed strangely empty—as if darkness, moon and stars had yet to be added to it. Jess seemed somewhat cooler than usual, seemed to emit less of a glow. As if he were withholding his warmth. In the dark she could not see the expression on his face.

"I have a fantasy," Karolina said, "of some magnetic force drawing everything I don't need from my life. Leaving it perfectly uncluttered." She did not look at him as she spoke. "Are there techniques," she asked, "for dealing with loss? I have lost so many things in my life."

"Yes, there are," he said.

"Then teach me," she said.

"Material things are not important," he said, "what matters is the sense of loss."

"No," she said, after a moment's reflection, "the things are important. Are there techniques for coping with this?"

"Yes, there are," he said.

"Can I make a list of the losses and forget about them afterwards—once and for all?"

"You can do that," he said.

"I have this fantasy of starting over again. A clean slate. No burdens. No regrets. No loose ends."

When they had almost reached the cemetery, they turned round, walking back along Johanna Brand Street. A light breeze sprang up. The night sky grew darker, deeper. The moon appeared. She thought she could sense again the heat emitted by the man beside her in the dark.

Jess came to a sudden halt beneath a tree. He turned towards her.

"What is the matter?" he asked.

She looked up at him, unable to reply straight away.

"I don't have your techniques to help me cope with unpleasant feelings," she said.

"Is that meant to be a reproach?" he asked.

"No," she said.

"I could teach you," he said. "Although I don't always manage to get it right myself."

"The road to bliss?" she asked.

"Why not?" he asked.

She could not see his eyes behind his glasses. She imagined if she should touch him now, she would burn her hand. Surely his body must be glowing like heated copper.

They continued their walk down Johanna Brand Street, as far as Stiebeuel Street, and from there back to the hotel.

When he said goodnight, he put his hand briefly on the back of her neck. Upstairs in her room—all night long—her neck and shoulders seemed to burn. The glow spread to the rest of her body. The soles of her feet and the palms of her hands seemed to burn so fiercely, she began to fear she might be coming down with something.

Tomorrow she would ask Basil to give her some remedy against the fever.

THE NEXT DAY she came upon the lovers in the Rendezvous Café when she went there for tea. It was a sombre day. The sky was grey, the atmosphere was stifling. Would it rain? They were sitting at a corner table against the left wall, under the window. A good place for lovers to meet, she thought, here in this dim corner, screened off from the rest of the café, safe from the relentless scrutiny of the townsfolk. Karolina sat down as inconspicuously as possible, ordered tea, and took a book on bats from her bag.

At close range the woman was even more beautiful than she had seemed from a distance. She was tall and delicate; she had a cloud of dark-brown hair and eyes like pools of water so clear as to allow one to see to the very bottom. Her companion, Jurie Beyers, was sunburnt, with short, dark hair and a prominent nose; there was an indefinable quality about him that could draw people to him irresistibly, Karolina thought. Something of this had already been apparent during his performance on stage—he seemed like someone who could charm people, who could twist them round his little finger. (His tragic fate in the play notwithstanding.)

But now they were here, smiling at each other. That is, the woman smiled a great deal, gazed up into her lover's eyes, stared down at the sugar bowl she was playing with. Karolina remembered the way she had sat on the night of the performance: tense, riveted to her seat, transported—as though her life depended on it. Her arms drawn protectively around her sleeping children.

Had Jurie Beyers staged the play for her benefit? Had the entire performance been an elaborate construct for the sake of this woman? Had he meant to convey a coded message to her? Why not choose something more appropriate then—something more erotic, less fateful? Who was she supposed to identify with—the poor murdered wife, trembling and insecure? Had there been a lesson intended for someone—for the man who was her lawful husband perhaps? Or did the play have no bearing at all on the lovers? Pure coincidence, peripheral to their passion.

How they smiled at each other now, how oblivious they were to everything! Nothing mattered but the moment, nothing leading up to it, and nothing that was to follow.

Once more Karolina remembered how the woman in the play had stood by the window. She had held onto the Moorish grid as if she were in jail, instead of in her bedroom with her bridegroom. She had gazed out of the window for such a long time that the audience had started to think something was amiss. And in the shadows surrounding the marital bed had stood her dark (artificially blackened) husband—consumed with conflicting emotions.

Karolina studied the snout of the hammerheaded fruit bat (*Hypsignathus monstrosus*) in the book before her. How she loved bats! Ever since she was a child. She had been fascinated by them for as long as she could remember. Neither mouse nor bird—an ambivalent creature. But her father's preference had been for insects, these had been the focus of his interest, his great passion, and he had soon won her over. She had admired and loved him, that is, before they had become alienated from each other.

The lovers spoke quietly, furtively. The woman's neck was very beautiful, and so were her ears. Perfectly cupped and receptive to the words he directed at her. She no longer seemed as distressed, as profoundly distressed, as on the first occasion in the cemetery.

In their presence Karolina suddenly experienced a keen emotion, akin to pain. The pain of being excluded. Excluded from the intimacy of the lovers' private domain, but also from the general realm of love. (Mercifully or not, she had yet to make out for herself.) She had emerged from the caravan, the sun had just gone down, she had almost tripped on a stone, she had laughed up her sleeve at the words of the woman with the gilded nest from which an enormous bird might ascend. And yet these very words had caused her ears to glow.

She rose to leave. The lovers looked in her direction, as if they had only just become aware of her intrusive presence. She paid at the cash register in the front section, bought a local paper, accepted a handbill from a child who was distributing them outside the café. She walked back to the hotel, this time paying no attention to the threatening sky that loomed over the church steeple behind her.

In the newspaper she found what she was after: an advertisement for a disco dance in a neighbouring town on Saturday night. (The town she had visited with Basil to collect the parcel for Mr. Quiroga.) Also a small news item concerning an accident involving a car and a pick-up truck that had taken place the previous week, and that had resulted in one person being injured and another killed. The deceased had been a prominent local lawyer, known mainly for the number of blacks he had defended.

ON SATURDAY EVENING Karolina went dancing in the neighbouring town, since she had need of something other than the usual. She said nothing at all of her intention to Basil or Jess. She took a different route from the one she and Basil had taken when they had come upon the scene of the accident.

She danced on her own into the early hours of the morning and drove back through a landscape shrouded in primordial mist. The graves of heroes were the only landmarks along the way. Exhausted, her mind a perfect blank, she drove through this silent, half-veiled landscape filled with graves and stone mounds dating back to the erstwhile Boer Republic.

After a night's dancing she would usually return tired out but content, her mind a blank, her calves numb. Occasionally something more would happen. While dancing she would unexpectedly enter a different plane of awareness. Whenever this happened she felt that all the years of dancing as if on hot coals had not been wasted. These experiences, however, were few and far between.

She drove through the hazy landscape in the hour immediately preceding sunrise. This desolate stretch of veld had been an arena of bitter conflict and bloodshed in the history of the country. Behind and to the right of her rose the mountain (obscured by the mist) where the Boers and the English had fought one of their bloody battles.

She slowed down—from the corner of her eye she had seen a sudden movement in the road ahead, some distance away. Thinking at first it must be an antelope, she made out a dark human form running across the road towards the right, pursued by two or three men. They proceeded down the steep embankment at the side of the road, then vanished into the veld, obscured by mist.

There was a stationary car on the left-hand side of the road, its doors thrown wide open. It looked like a police car, and a single passenger was seated in the back. Her heart beat uncontrollably. Immediately after she had passed the point where the men had run across the road, one, two, three shots rang out behind her, then the gentle silence descended once again, on this erstwhile place of confrontation.

CHAPTER 5

WHEN KAROLINA came into the ladies' bar on Monday evening, Pol was at a corner table with his friends, singing "The Lady with the Little Red Dress." Every word, every syllable, salaciously charged. His back was turned—as usual—to the now absent magistrate.

She sat down at the bar counter. Pol's suggestive revelry had set her nerve-ends tingling. But she sat perfectly still, giving no indication of her mood.

Pol came up to her, glass in hand. He wiped his wet face with a handkerchief; his body heat was so much greater than anyone else's.

He said nothing at first. Merely tilted his head and gazed at her.

Here was a man who must be halfway transformed to something amphibian, she thought.

"So," he said gravely. "How is the young lady?"

"I'm well," said Karolina, "or reasonably well."

He continued his close scrutiny of her, head tilted to one side. The whites of the elongated, watery eyes long since grown invisible. The mouth narrow and wet. Gills growing behind the ears. She liked him.

"Where have you been, all the days of my life?" he asked.

"Listen, Pol," she said softly, lowering her head so she could speak close to his ear. "Do you know about the man who was killed in the accident on the way to Volksrust. The lawyer?"

"Yes, I know about him," said Pol. Cautiously.

"Will someone be investigating his death?" asked Karolina.

"No," said Pol. He bent his head towards her. "We don't look for shit around here," he said. "We don't ask to be rapped over the knuckles." He turned his gaze slowly in the direction of the (absent) magistrate. "We don't want to provoke that lad." They both looked at the empty chair for a moment. He gave a slight shudder. He took a sip from his glass. "Or our very own captain in there," he said, indicating the snooker room with his head. "The one doesn't want to get his hands dirty," gesturing in the direction of the absent magistrate, "and the other one can't get them dirty enough."

"Do you know if anyone was shot in this area at the weekend?" she asked.

Pol looked at her attentively with the watery eyes, his expression unfathomable. He shrugged in mute reply.

"One might be able to find out," he said.

"Is there no one in this town who opposes them?" she asked.

Pol studied her at length. "Ever heard of the Delarey and Beyers Theatrical Company?" he asked, giving her a meaningful look. "*The Jealous Husband* and all that crap," he said, smiling his impenetrable, amphibian smile. "After all, we did turn up to a man to show our support."

Karolina smiled. Looked down into her glass. Smiled, shook her head, continued to smile.

"You still have to tell me of the great battle that was fought around here," she said.

"I grow cold when I think of everything I shall be telling you still," he said, and shuddered violently.

They took leave of each other and Karolina went back to her room without looking left or right, in the direction of the absent magistrate or the snooker room. Up the baroque staircase, feeling the silky smooth handrail under the palm of her hand.

My God, she thought, what an elaborate cover.

A MAN WHO had never been well disposed towards her turned up in a dream. He had been sent by someone else, by someone she had loved all her life, across great distances even, but who had never returned her love. (One of her two unrequited loves.) This man met her on a campus, where she had come to find a lost handbag. He then took her on an outing to a tearoom. As happens in dreams, the environment was changed subtly, but beyond recognition.

So, your work—he said. Karolina interrupted him—I have nobody that loves me, she said. The man took her hand, palpated and examined it. A strong pulse, there is a lot of sap in your marrow, he said.

How strange that he should fail to see that her hand was worn thin with despondency, Karolina thought in her dream.

SHE DREAMT a close friend (who had died some years ago) was alive again. She was back in their midst. Returned to the living. She had returned to her husband, returned to her children; pregnant, planning for the future. Ready, available, fully restored. The ten or more years since her decease left behind.

ON WEDNESDAY morning Karolina and Basil drove to Wakkerspruit, a small dorp about seventy kilometres directly east of Voorspoed. (Four weeks to the day since she had first set out for Voorspoed; since she had first met Basil; since she had had her palm read in the caravan.) They were going to collect another parcel for Mr. Quiroga. This road, too, took them past Majuba Mountain, where the Boers had defeated the English in 1881.

Wakkerspruit was a very small place. The main street was a through road, the only one that was tarred; the rest of the town consisted of no more than a few wide dirt roads. They collected Mr. Quiroga's parcel from someone in an old house next to the post office. There were cypresses, apricot trees and pink stocks in the front garden, and a type of lawn that Karolina associated with the lawns of her childhood—she also remembered this from her visits to Voorspoed in the days of her sleepy innocence, more than twenty-five years ago.

She sat in the car, waited for Basil. She looked at her hand. She felt her pulse. She remembered the dream. A lot of sap in her marrow?!

She was suddenly overcome by a feeling of disquiet. She had to walk; she was like a dog that had picked up an old, familiar scent.

When Basil came back with the parcel, they walked. In the centre of the town was a square with a stone church. To the north and east of the square was a single row of white-owned shops. To the south of it was the Coloured part of town, including a small number of Indian stores. To the west was the white residential area.

They passed a hairdresser's salon where Karolina went in to look for a hairbrush. (Her brush had snapped that morning.) The salon was a single, spacious room with chairs and mirrors along one wall, a sofa against the opposite wall, a table in the centre, with a sewing machine on top. No customers. She was assisted by the chirpy owner in a little overdress in two shades of mauve. Karolina chose a brush and paid at the counter. The woman wrote in her appointment book: 11h00, one brush. No other entries for the day as yet.

The shop to the left of the hairdresser's must have closed down recently. There were boards nailed over the door, a potted plant that still had to be removed on the wide windowsill.

It seemed some of these shops would be in business one day—albeit with dwindling supplies and empty shelves—and would have their doors boarded up the next.

Karolina and Basil passed the Bits&Pieces shop. The proprietor and his wife sat behind the counter. His head was only just visible, hers quite out of sight. A mantel clock in the shape of a fountain stood guard on a shelf above their heads. The man was playing with a pink leather flyswatter while he waited for customers. (Ready to swat them to death?) His wife was smoking rhythmically, one cigarette after another. The tiny smoke rings she blew ascended straight to heaven.

They passed Magdalena Oberholzer's butcher's shop. Magdalena was hacking and grinding away inside, dressed in a dainty frock with a frilly collar and wearing a pair of glasses with a saucy trim on the frame.

They passed a secondhand furniture shop. Its door also boarded up and nailed shut.

Here Karolina stood riveted to the spot—fascinated. In one of the two display windows there was a dummy dressed up in a yellowed bridal gown. She stood before a wardrobe that had been pushed up against the window, its back facing outwards, so that the contents of the rest of the small shop were no longer clearly visible from the outside. As if some drama were being enacted in the dark, concealed part of the shop, the neglected bride providing a sombre clue to its theme. A portent, perhaps, in the way brides in dreams were often harbingers of death.

Karolina stared into the darkened, half-hidden shop interior as if it were a screen on which the hidden contents of her own mind were being projected.

The name of the place was Kallie's Secondhand Store. God alone knew where Kallie might be. Out to lunch? A protracted lunch. A never-ending picnic. A journey, a trip, an adventure from which Kallie might return only in the early part of the third millennium, when the maize and the wheat were green upon the fields again. When the town would have entered upon a new cycle of heedlessness. When times of drought, unrest, disaster and misery would have been left behind. Perhaps Kallie had gone underground. Blind as a mole. Perhaps he was hibernating along with his wife and his children—a season of psychedelic hibernation under the floorboards. Kallie would rise again.

Outside the store a young black woman was leaning against a post supporting the verandah, talking to a black man. Unmoved by the decayed white bride in the window or the invisible contents of the boarded-up shop.

Let's get out of here, Karolina said to Basil. Behind them the church bell tolled. A large number of cars were parked outside the church. A wedding, Karolina thought at first, then she saw the hearse parked at an angle behind the church.

They walked across the square, past the church, towards the post office. Outside the church was a pile of stones commemorating the fallen Boers.

Inside the church lay the local social worker, who had died by her own hand, the girl in the post office informed them when Basil bought some postage stamps.

A low mountain rose before them, to the west. On the slope an ox-wagon and the dates 1838–1939 were laid out in white-washed stones. The mountain seemed invitingly green, the surrounding landscape fresh, as they drove back.

"Probably only the old and the poor have remained behind in this town," said Karolina. "The rest of them must all have moved off to the city by now."

The landscape remained beautiful in spite of the drought. Karolina had an urge to lie stretched out on one of the low hills. So she might draw strength from the earth and into the marrow of her bones. So she might be filled once again with the undifferentiated life force of a young child on the verge of maturity.

It was Jess she was thinking of during the rest of the journey home.

SHE WENT TO PLAY snooker that same evening. (Karolina could not stay away for long.) The ladies' bar was practically deserted: one or two couples, a few unfamiliar faces. Pol and the magistrate notably absent.

Kieliemann was in the snooker room (he seemed perfectly impassive when she came in), flat-faced Boet Visagie was there, the two teachers—Baluschagne and Kriek—were there, as were the two FAK individuals, Sergeant Frikkie, and a few reps. It was the middle of the week, a quiet evening. Conditions were less favourable for the unravelling of psyches, for the stirring up of unruly emotions. What lurked beneath the surface would remain there. The potential for violence on all levels was smaller. Balletjies would not be giving an account of the extraordinary size of his cock tonight. Captain Gert Els would not be coming into the room to issue urgent instructions for a raid, a foray, for anything requiring immediate punitive action.

The game was subdued, the tone of the conversation even. The teachers in the corner spoke of racing pigeons, the reps spoke of new dipping fluids, irrigation pumps. There was talk about the weather, local affairs, guns.

Karolina endured Kieliemann's casual touch, his hand on her buttocks now and then. She kept her ears pricked up, but there was no mention of the visit to the township the previous week, and even less of the shooting incident at the weekend. No mention of anything untoward. Not a word to give any indication that things were constantly brewing underneath the surface.

The disquiet that had come over Karolina did not leave her. When she had arrived here a month ago, she had been complete and content—or so she had thought. Now she had to laugh sometimes at the improbable nature of the knowledge she was being initiated into by Basil every day. The things the woman in the rococo caravan had told her seemed even more farfetched, and she had laughed at those as well.

Even so she was in a state of heightened expectation. She was waiting for something to happen. As if she had well and truly taken the woman's absurd predictions to heart. As if they had become some sort of signpost to her. The more she tried to shake off the sense of anticipation, the greater her impatience and her sense of disquiet. And the less she was able to continue her life as it had been—devoted to the study of moths, successfully removed from the sphere of emotional entanglement.

She had quite deliberately placed herself outside this sphere years ago, after coming to her senses in a hotel room one night. (There had been a railway track on the other side of the road.) Having decided that this was it. The end of a season. Of an era of courting disaster. So much for indiscretion and reckless living, with no thought to the consequences. She had risen from the cooling bedsheets immediately, but had already paid dearly.

It had been too late for some things. She and her father had already been alienated from each other. But other things had remained. She had been able to return to the foundations of knowledge that had been imparted to her at an early age. The old passion had been there still. It had been there for her on her return: the twenty-nine orders.

Her parents were dead. Her mother had died before her father—too soon, much too soon. Her only sister lived in one of the remotest corners of the world—it seemed she could hardly remove herself far enough from human proximity.

Nothing but the dance remained to connect Karolina—by the most tenuous of threads—to the deepest, most passionate, unfettered aspects of her psyche. Only within the narrowly circumscribed movements of the dance could she (on rare and unexpected occasions) raise the column of liquid fire in her spine, and experience a strange, impersonal ecstasy.

Karolina sat on the cane seat in the corner. She surveyed the scene. From the other side of the room Kieliemann was keeping a constant watch on her. When her turn came, she played her shot. She drank her whisky. She felt as if she were on fire, she felt like dancing the tarantella, naked, in full view of everyone here, on hot coals on the green, burning surface of the snooker table.

ON SATURDAY EVENING she played snooker again. Basil accompanied her. It was a warm night, a hot wind stirred in the streets. The village dogs howled at the moon. Everybody seemed to be at the hotel tonight.

From early on the atmosphere was charged with menace. As if everyone present were walking around with bleeding gums caused by unspeakable deprivation.

Pol sang more heartily than ever in the ladies' bar tonight: "When I Was a Mere Schoolboy." The magistrate's whorish neigh rang out above Pol's sonorous bass, alternately counterpointing and subverting it. Patrons were sitting shoulder to shoulder at the bar counter or crowding round the oasis of the snooker table. Everything adrift and male and hungry or thirsty was driven to this place tonight by the warm wind and the full moon.

Basil constantly wiped the sweat from his brow, drank his beer, but remained as unruffled as ever. Karolina's shoulders, bare and delicately curved tonight, glistened with a fine layer of sweat. Her dark hair was charged with electricity—every hair seemed to spring up from its follicle with a vigorous life of its own.

When they were not playing, she sat next to Basil on the cane seat in the corner, immediately to the right of the door leading to the ladies' bar. She questioned him about those present. They spoke quietly, cautiously, despite the tremendous din in the room.

Karolina drank whisky. How did everyone manage to keep up this frenzied pace—travelling salesmen, policemen, teachers, farmers? As the evening wore on everyone—so it seemed—was moving on the verge of altered states, sliding in and out of bizarre perceptions. Facilitated by the consumption of alcohol, by the mesmerising green surface of the snooker table, by the yellow walls, by the endless talk, and by a compelling larger rhythm which dictated the movements of all those present.

Other nights seemed more loosely woven by comparison. Those present constantly drifted apart and came together again to form new combinations, their ceaseless movement and random grouping meshed together by the surreal effect of the light and by the crazy talk—cunt and cock talk, drought talk, bullshit talk.

Though he sat in an easy chair all night, smoking, drinking and laughing, even the magistrate in the ladies' bar next door was part of this pattern of breaking up and coming together. Though the pitch of his laughter rose constantly and his incessant chatter grew increasingly unintelligible, still he remained part—like Basil and Karolina and Pol, like all those present—of the slow, undanced dance that was being performed round the table and in the wings.

As the evening and the night and the moon progressed, everyone displayed amphibian characteristics (not only Pol, who was already there, swimming along, regardless of the outcome). As the blood grew colder, so the chill in the veins had to be countered incessantly by the consumption of fiery liquid. (So, for instance, a sense of worthlessness, of a loss of vitality and of prospects grew in the younger De Melck brother—despite the powerful breeding potential of his Hereford stud, and despite the autistic redhead—hair the shade of a Rhode Island Red—to whom he was lawfully joined in marriage, or possibly in some measure because of her.) As the blood grew colder, or unbearably hot, so the repressed psychic contents broke free from their murky sediment, and floated slowly to the surface—the underlying anxieties, the countless senseless schemes and impulses, the dreams of bountiful maternal breasts. The threatening feelings of vulnerability, manifested by an increased sensitivity of the genitals, rose. As did the excessive feelings of guilt, the lurking fear of sudden, loud noises, of fire, of large, shiny, shimmering surfaces, of suffocation, of disease, of insanity, of the unknown.

The magistrate sat in the ladies' bar, too fastidious to dirty his own hands. Pol was singing "All the Veld Rejoices." Mr. Kriek's cheeks glowed, the golden-haired De Melck brother's resolve was growing and Balls's strategies were taking shape almost visibly. Karolina's head was spinning, the walls expanded and contracted, emitting a sulphurous yellow glow.

Basil took her gently but firmly by the arm—it's late, hadn't she better be going to bed, he said. They did not walk through the ladies' bar, but went out through the door leading to the toilets (where Gert Els had made his first appearance), passed through the dining room (deserted now, under the panels), and crossed the lounge (where the dejected husband had taken the blow like a gentleman) to the reception area in all its sensual, oaken, carved, baroque glory. At Karolina's request they went out on the stoep for a breath of fresh air. The night was warm, but it was still considerably cooler outside than inside. She remained there with Basil for a while, the cool night air on her cheeks wonderfully refreshing.

Then Basil, courteous as ever, wished her a good night. He walked off to his room in the upper part of town, under the roof of the remarkable Mr. Quiroga. She had to find other lodgings, she could not remain here any longer, she thought. She was never at peace here, her energies were wasted.

Turning to go inside, she started—she had not seen him. Although Jess's friend Frans Roeg was sitting in the dark at a small, solitary table, he was quite visible by the light of the moon. On the table before him were a bottle and a glass.

There was a strange expression on his face—both inviting and rejecting. She wanted to go up to him, sit down next to him, speak to him. At the same time she shrank back from something forbidding about him.

She hesitated for no more than a moment, nodded briefly in his direction, went into the hotel and rapidly up the stairs, the polished satinwood handrail cool under her fiery palm.

As she was about to go to sleep there was a light tap on her door. Immediately she was wide awake, but she decided to ignore it. When the knock was not repeated she relaxed, and fell asleep shortly afterwards.

During the night she dreamt that she had had enough of living over the fridges of the dead—it seemed there was a place down below where the dead were hatching in fridges. This place, this underground, was alive—it extended over a vast area and there were ventilation shafts leading to the surface above.

She had lively, lusty, confusing dreams. Men she knew and did not know appeared in them. One man in particular was singled out as the embodiment of her desire—he was the one who would satisfy her. But time and again satisfaction was postponed, delayed, frustrated, impeded, thwarted, until at last her desire became painfully acute, a situation she had to escape from at all costs. The dream with all its various strategies was directed entirely to this end, serving simultaneously to distract and to gratify.

THE NEXT MORNING, which was Sunday, Jess took her out for a drive. He had come to the hotel to look for her. They had tea at the local dam that had been converted to a pleasure resort; they sat at a stone table under an umbrella. Since it was off-season, the place was virtually deserted. She would have liked to sit closer to the water's edge, under the willow trees, where they had picnicked years ago. She remembered it well. But there was an entirely different feel to the place now.

It was a cloudy day. Bothasberg lay in the distance, with a vast, gentle, brown and pink plain between the mountain and the water. The clouds cast huge shadows on this plain, and it was dotted with small clusters of bluegum trees. The day was cool after the heat of the last few days. It seemed as if she hadn't seen Jess for a long time.

What had she been doing all week, he asked. Mostly working at her research in the mornings, she said; going to Wakkerspruit with Basil to collect a parcel for Mr. Quiroga; playing a little snooker at night. She asked how his research was coming on. Well, he said, he had put in quite an effort the past week.

"What's become of your friend Frans?" she asked.

"I haven't seen much of him lately," Jess said. "He came round last night. He is not very happy right now. But then he never really opens up to me. I suspect there's a dark, reserved side to him—but this may well be projection on my part. He's in a difficult relationship, I think."

Karolina looked out dreamily on the outstretched plain, the landscape unspoilt from this distance.

"He's like someone who has dreams of purity that arise from within his darkest impulses. A yearning for something unsullied in himself, as opposed to something brutal and treacherous." Jess paused, then continued. "Perhaps I'm saying more about myself than about him."

Karolina was watching Jess, he would look down when he spoke, he seemed embarrassed every time he looked up.

"Do you know the woman he's involved with?" she asked.

"No," he said. "I've seen her with him a couple of times. She's very beautiful. One of the most beautiful women I've ever seen. Though it seems she's not doing very well either, right now."

They drank their tea in silence.

"Does Frans interest you?" Jess asked suddenly.

Karolina shrugged. "Not particularly," she said. "He didn't seem very happy. I wondered what sort of person he was." She looked at the trees along the water's edge. Had there always been so few of them?

"Tell me more about your research," she said.

As he spoke, she observed him closely, unobtrusively from behind her dark glasses. She found him a strange mixture of inconsistencies—the heat emitted by his skin, and the cool, almost aloofness of his manner. An obtrusive sensuality, and at the same time a suggestion of mortality. (Because he showed a more open concern with death than most people? Because he did not deny death's reality, but nevertheless offered her his warmth like a gift?) The more he seemed to elude her, the brighter his glow. The more she tried to deny the warm tangibility of his presence, the more powerfully she could sense the nature of her surrender. She felt her ligaments slacken like those of a pregnant woman. It can't be very long now, she thought.

They drove back through the mellow landscape and he dropped her off outside the hotel. Since she had refused his invitation to lunch, she ate by herself under the painted panels in the dining room.

CHAPTER 6

ONLY FOUR of the six painted panels in the dining room were actually panels of confrontation. The other two were nostalgic panels depicting an idyllic life.

Nobody could tell Karolina who the artist was and when the panels had been painted. Nobody at the hotel knew who had commissioned them, whose idea it had been to highlight these particular events from local history. Just as no one knew anything about the history of the baroque reception desk and the magnificent staircase.

As the hotel was under new management, the woman at the reception desk—with hoarse voice and sharp eye—said she couldn't say who might have decorated the hotel in the past.

But whoever the artist, the six panels were inspired. Even the two panels of idyllic life had an atmosphere of impending disaster to them—paradise within hours of the fall, the fragile balance of unspoilt nature on the verge of being disturbed. In the painted skies delicate intimations of disaster could already be discerned: a rosy sky tending toward bloody red; a tiny smear of grey in a cloud, suggesting smoke and fire.

The four panels of confrontation portrayed the Battle of Majuba, the Siege of Ladysmith, the Battle of Isandlwana, and a white punitive raid on a black kraal.

In these panels the entire cosmos was drawn into the fray. In the Battle of Majuba (Place of the Doves) there was a delicate but unmistakeable explosion of supernovae in the sky, with a cloud like an omen on the top of the hill—a suitable backdrop for the Second Coming. In the Siege of Ladysmith the sky was filled with exploding meteorites and comets, spectacular celestial phenomena. In the attack on a black kraal an immense sky filled with towering masses of cloud dominated a vast, nostalgic landscape of golden red cliffs that plunged away into mists and deep crevices—with tiny, soft trees in the infinite distance. The small group of whites in the foreground and the stronghold in the middle ground hardly visible.

In each of the panels human activity was reduced to insignificance, dwarfed by the presence of nature. The landscape was the great constant, the human groups moving across it were small and irrelevant, insignificant, coincidental, peripheral. The mountains in the background were old, older than human history. They reached back deep into the geological periods of the Cretaceous, the Jurassic, the Triassic. The artist had indeed had a powerful vision, an ability to evoke within a single panel the prehistory of the region as well as a particular historical incident.

The panels were large, the colours rusty red, ochre, pale yellow, and a washed-out indigo blue. They were painted in a nineteenth century heroic style. Small groups of people were doing their level best—in the foreground, in the middle distance, on the vast plains and under the faded, blue, ancient hills and mountain ranges in the background—to offer their paltry contribution to the history of the making of this land.

And who might get to see these panels? Voorspoed was not a large town, and it was not on a major route connecting the larger centres and the cities. The few reps and travellers who stayed over at the hotel? The solitary visitors who happened to stray into the hotel? It was touch and go, and she might have missed out on them too, and then she might never have been afforded this perspective on history, Karolina thought.

WHEN SHE WAS on her own, Karolina speculated endlessly on Delarey and Beyers.

If Pol's insinuations were true, if Delarey and Beyers were indeed implicated in some other activity, why had they put on the play?

The audience, too, had been visibly uncertain of what had hit them. What were they to make of the artificially blackened husband, of the father-in-law as raging bull (sexually possessive of his daughter)? The company had played unerringly on the raw nerve-end, on a slight uncertainty on the part of the audience. Everybody had been thrown off balance, caught off guard—had they not huddled together round the cake tables during the interval like a flock of bewildered sheep? All, of course, but Pol, can of Coke (filled with brandy) in one hand, koeksister in the other. (A conspiratorial wink at Karolina.) And what of the lover in the third row from the front? Riveted to her seat, her expression (in the dark, in profile) rapt, alarmed; her arms protectively round her two sleeping children. Was her husband at her side consumed with jealousy, despite being in full control on the face of it? (Always a man of breeding.) And the local farmers, and the townsfolk, and the few township residents, the collective asthmatic wheezing and the general coughing and sputtering, interspersed with moments of silence so profound one might have heard the drop of a mouse turd.

Were Delarey and Beyers acting according to a double agenda; was the entire play a complex coded message?

"What do you make of them, Basil?" asked Karolina. "What do you make of Jurie Beyers? What do you think he's hoping to achieve?"

But Basil was evasive. Karolina began to suspect he knew more than he was prepared to disclose. She did not pursue the matter.

She and Basil sat under the willow tree, in the lovely shade. They ate their sandwiches, drank tea from a Thermos. Karolina thought of the two men. They had caught her imagination. She had her hopes on them.

ON SATURDAY NIGHT Karolina danced with the Kolyn fellow again in the dining room of the hotel. First she drank orange squash with ice on the stoep. She surveyed the night sky for signs of cosmic disruption, the portentous movement of stars and comets, mindful of the painted panels she would shortly be dancing under. Inside, the band was warming up like locusts before a migratory flight.

The Kolyn fellow hovered in the background like a large, limp water lily. His testicles cold and wilted. His calves bulging, the long, narrow feet shod in lace-up sneakers. The dark eyes constantly watchful.

He rose and asked her to dance. Soon they were moving across the floor at a firm pace. His timing was perfect, her style unsurpassable, they did not speak, she stared fixedly over his right shoulder. His right hand clasped her waist securely, but his left hand was unaccountably listless.

Karolina deliberately shut out the clamour of the snooker room: she had decided to stay away from it for the time being.

Round and round the Kolyn fellow swept her, round and round the dining room, past the painted panels high up on the wall above them. Past the Battle of Majuba, past the Siege of Ladysmith, past the Battle of Isandlwana. They danced well—their movements were effortless, their footwork superb, their timing impeccable. Along with the other couples they did the *louche*, the unbearably sensual tango—underneath the painted scenes from the history of the struggle for possession and control of the soil beneath their feet.

Among the dancing couples not a single head was raised in remembrance of the fallen dead, of the sacrifice of those fallen in battle in the faded light of these momentous landscapes. Each one had his gaze fixed firmly on his own dark future.

CHAPTER 7

EVERY AFTERNOON Karolina would lie on her bed; she would dream, wonder, speculate, fantasise. She would slip into and out of dreams, she would speculate on the occurrence and distribution of the evasive moths, on the deceitful pair Delarey and Beyers. She would wonder about the lovers, the beautiful woman and the charismatic man. What did they say to each other, how did he make love to her? She would have liked to be a fly on the wall so she could take a closer, unobserved look at Jurie Beyers and Manie Delarey. She wanted to hear what they said and to see what they did. She lay on her bed, linked to no one and to everyone. She was free of hindrances, she moved about wherever she wished. She stayed with the moths, she stayed with the men; she stayed briefly, uneasily, with Jess. She stared at the palms of her hands. She stared unseeingly at the ceiling. A recurring fantasy came to her. It seemed to intrude on her from outside—more an omen than a fantasy. It centred on Captain Gert Els. The broad outlines of the scene that came to her were as follows. She wakes up in the night, and there is someone by her bed. In the dark an object is held to her head like a weapon. It is his penis. He threatens her with it. She must do whatever he wishes or commands. Sometimes the magistrate sits on the other side of the bed. He is a silent accomplice.

IT WAS THE seventh week of her stay in the town, mid-February and ferociously hot. The drought had entered its mature phase.

The farmers were desperate, said the reps in the dining room. Only the wealthiest were still holding out, farmers like the brothers De Melck. The numbers of the hopeless were swelling ominously. Gangs of black and white marauders were roaming the area, the salesmen reported.

Police reinforcements would be brought to the town, said the owner of the Springbok Café where Karolina and Basil bought their sandwiches every morning.

The people in the location have been at each other's throats again, the Kolyn fellow told Karolina while they were taking a break between dances on the cool stoep on Saturday night. (Four weeks after the incident in the township.) How is it you know so much about it? she asked him. Oh, one picks up these things when one happens to be in town, he replied. And have you managed to come up with some sort of aid for the farmers? she asked. We-ell, he said, we do what we can, but we're up against something terrible here, a terrible drought—the government is having a bloody hard time, trying to help out everybody everywhere. And what else is happening in the township? she asked. But he clammed up suddenly, and during the next round he swept her round the floor more furiously than before.

WHAT HAD BECOME of the men she had loved, Karolina wondered, the men she had thought she loved? One had flown away on enormous black wings. One had gone underground to wrestle with forces and demons that would bar his way to the surface for as long as he should live. One had remained above ground and resolutely done his duty. The first, a youthful love, had set out unswervingly on a course of suckling at the breast of a powerful surrogate mother.

And what of her two unrequited loves? One lived on in her conscious mind like sand in the soft flesh of an oyster—but no pearl would ever come of it. The other appeared in her dreams in many different guises: severe, rejecting, loving, inviting, indifferent. Each time he would be performing some strange task—chopping meat, or pruning trees, or addressing a public gathering, or making a bed.

The rest had plunged down the abyss like a herd of swine—some more and some less deserving, but each one of them essentially meaningless within the constellation of Karolina's psyche.

TOWARDS FRIDAY EVENING Karolina gave up on her resolution to keep away from the snooker room. She had a drink in the ladies' bar first. Pol came up to her. I've been hearing all sorts of things about the township, she said to him. What's going on there?

He remained silent for a little while before glancing furtively around the room to make sure no one was looking in their direction. (No one was—everyone was carrying on his own conversation, acting out or repressing his own fantasies.) Only then did Pol incline his head dramatically towards her ear, saying softly: "Can you keep a secret?"

"I can," she said, speaking quietly too, close to his ear.

"Our very own captain," he said, indicating the snooker room with his head, as if Gert Els were one of its permanent fixtures, "has made it clear from the very beginning that he would not tolerate a branch of the ANC here. He would see to it himself." Pol moved even closer to Karolina. She felt the hot, moist steam he emitted on her skin. "He was the one who first organised a group of gangsters to attack the people, and then hired a black hit squad to try and kill off the leaders."

"How do you know this?" asked Karolina.

"I know because I go through life with my eyes and ears wide open," said Pol. "One could say every single one of my very own senses is always on full alert."

He fixed his unfathomable and watery gaze on her, wiped his face with a handkerchief. "I shudder to think of all the things my senses are still to discover!" he said, shuddering visibly.

Karolina remembered the contemptuous way in which Gert Els had scraped his boot clean on the steps as he emerged from the house of the man in the township.

"But what of Beyers and Delarey, what are they doing to stop him?" she asked.

"A cunning pair," he said. "Those lads move in silent and mysterious ways, like the Holy Ghost."

"So why make themselves so visible? What if Gert Els should get to them?"

Pol shrugged dramatically. He spread his hands, palms turned upward: "They weren't born yesterday," he said. "Don't worry—they won't allow that bonehead to get hold of them." He swallowed down some liquor. He looked at Karolina long and affectionately. "You saw what they were up to on the stage that night."

"What were they up to?" she asked.

"Nothing was what it seemed." Once again Pol paused significantly. "Only the tea and the koeksisters were truly, inalienably themselves."

Karolina, feeling somewhat comforted by this, parted from Pol and took on the snooker room.

Shortly afterwards she heard him singing heartily in the room next door: 'I love silver, I love gold.' Her eye fell on the golden Tonnie, the radiantly blond younger De Melck brother. His face was flushed, as if warmly suffused with blood—a troubled face.

Kieliemann remained straight-faced, but spared no effort in trying to make up for time lost during the week or so that she had abstained from playing snooker.

Despite the ceiling fan, everyone was dripping with perspiration—the heat was so intense. Karolina played with determination, but with a feeling of constriction in her throat. She drank whisky. The green landscape of the tabletop seemed toxic. Her temples throbbed, her face was unnaturally hot. Kieliemann was breathing in her neck, his hands were on her buttocks, they were all over every part of her that he could get hold of without being seen, the taut Terylene bulge pressed furiously against her at every opportunity. Karolina allowed him to carry on unchecked, too caught up in her own sensations to be fighting him off all the time. She both recognised and denied her own excitement at the thought of Jess.

As usual, Kieliemann barred her way in the little passage as she came out of the ladies' toilet. Without further ado he pinned her to the wall. She tried to slip out of his grip, exasperated. But he was more passionate than usual tonight.

"Let me go, Kieliemann!" she said, "I want to get back to the game!"

But Kieliemann's mouth was wet and persistent in her neck, his hands reached everywhere. He was short, sturdy, with narrow slit eyes and an oily skin. He breathed heavily. A notorious fist fighter by day, given to bursts of rage.

"Why don't you rather tell me what's going on in the township?" she said as she tried to free herself from his grip.

At that moment the door leading to the dining room was opened and Manie Delarey came out into the passage, on his way to the toilet, most likely. Kieliemann promptly let go of Karolina. She stared in bewilderment at the man, who barely glanced at her as he passed.

She was furious with Kieliemann. In the toilet she washed her hands and splashed water on her face. Were they both here—Jurie Beyers too? She did not feel like going back to the snooker room, deciding to go to the ladies' bar instead.

As she entered she saw them straight away. Jurie Beyers and Manie Delarey were at one of the low round tables, and they were not alone. There were two women with them. One of them seemed to be the woman who had played the murdered wife (minus the long blond wig), the other the woman who had played the traitorous friend.

They all looked up briefly when Karolina came into the room. She felt a certain embarrassment, but she decided what the hell, she would sit there even if they took her for the local tart. She would sit down where she could observe them. Pol was no longer there, or she would have joined him.

Both women were of indeterminate age—in their mid-thirties, by the look of it. The one who had played the white bride had dark hair; she was intense, she smoked excessively, she was so nervous the tips of her fingers seemed almost to quiver. The other had shoulders that were conspicuously bare in a loose-fitting summer dress. A skin like peaches—soft and velvety. Beautiful shoulders, sexy, but something vicious about the face.

Both women looked as if they might hold firm opinions, have formulated world views, subscribe to specific moral codes (the bride more particularly so) and both seemed to exude a formidable eroticism (the vicious one more particularly so). The four of them were engaged in lively, intense conversation. Not the usual loose and flirtatious bar talk.

If they were devising schemes, discussing strategies, why here, the hottest nest in town, headquarters of Gert Els and company? Shouldn't they be keeping a somewhat lower profile? She felt she had no idea what was going on here. Perhaps Pol's mind was so blown, perhaps his amphibious transformation was so near complete that the fabrications of his subaquatic imagination were beginning to seem real to him. Perhaps they were indeed no more than a band of strolling players, and perhaps the faith she had placed in them had been unjustified.

She felt excluded once again, as she had felt in the café, in the presence of the lovers. She literally felt like a loose woman tonight—severed from all meaningful human ties. She reminded herself that her own intentions and choices had brought her to this point, and not some force of destiny.

Some time later she went up to her room, following the worn carpet down the passage. She lay down across the bed, sniffed at the cool sheets. Not a trace of the body odour and heat she longed for.

DURING THE NIGHT Karolina was half awakened by voices in the passage outside her room.

"The fucking dog got away," somebody said. (The magistrate's voice?)

She turned over, heavy with sleep, and continued to dream.

THERE WAS NO sign of the travelling players on Sunday morning—not in the passages, the dining room, the lounge or on the hotel stoep. They must have moved on again.

It was a fine morning and Jess turned up to ask her out for a walk. They walked towards the centre of town first, then turned left towards the older, leafier part, right to the very top, where the houses bordered on the veld. It was hot and they walked slowly, in the shade of the trees whenever possible. The trees cast deep shadows on Jess's heated shape.

Her physical sensations in his presence were of a very specific nature today—sweaty palms, a heightened sense of smell, a restless anticipation, almost to the point of irritability. Jess showed no unusual symptoms, he kept his eyes lowered as they walked.

She questioned him about the Buddhist attitude to death. He explained. She wanted to know more. He explained that the mind should always be open—it should merely observe; like a mirror, reflecting only that which is. Only the present is important. To be aware, one's head should preferably be quite empty, he said with a self-conscious little laugh.

"Do you manage to do all of this?" she asked.

"Better at some times than at others," he said.

As they walked along, she had a growing sense of weightlessness, she seemed to grow lighter, he seemed to become heavier.

One should reflect on death all the time, he said. In the morning, in the afternoon, in the evening. An early Ka-Dam-Pa master said that if one should wake up in the morning and find that one is not meditating on death, the morning will have been wasted. Likewise the afternoon and the evening. Death should not come as a surprise. One should not feel regret in the face of death.

She listened in silence.

He invited her to his room for tea. He rented a room in the upper part of town from an old couple who lived in a large old house in Sipres Avenue. (Karolina imagined she recognised the house.) His room was large and bright, and it contained nothing but a bed, a table, two chairs and a wardrobe.

He sat down in one chair, she sat down in the other. There was a pile of books on the table. The book with the flaming red cover lay right on top. The floors were of pale wood. There was a white cover on the bed. The thin lace curtains were white, they stirred lightly in the breeze. The heavy outer curtains, now open, were cream.

They sat facing each other rather miserably. (Karolina was shivering slightly.) Until Jess got up, drew her close to him and muttered in her hair (somewhat indistinctly): From the moment I first set eyes on you. Karolina laughed (softly) and allowed him to put an end to her misery.

CHAPTER 8

KAROLINA HAD burnt all her things before coming here. She had attempted to rid herself of everything she considered superfluous to her life. A pall of smoke had hung over the city every day. Despite the whirring of the fans, the heat had remained palpable. Over the promenade along the seafront the night sky had turned yellow, and the palm trees swayed in the wind. She had saved a few letters, the rest she had burnt.

In the veld with Basil, Karolina was restored to her childhood sense of self. Here she seldom felt unformed, or incomplete.

Basil did not speak much. They spent long hours together without saying much. Now and then he would tell her something about himself. Mostly he would merely point out things. She asked him once whether there was someone that he loved and he said yes, there was.

She asked him how he had first met Mr. Quiroga and how he had come to the study of natural remedies. He told her he had left the country with some other people in the seventies. They had been tracked down in Botswana. He had jumped from a moving truck and had been shot at. He had been badly wounded and left behind for dead. A small band of desert people had found him. They had rubbed a thick layer of animal fat into his body, rolled him in mud, and covered him with leaves. He had been left to lie like that for a long time. They had nursed him back to health. These were the people who had first taught him about indigenous medicines. He had come to hear of Mr. Quiroga much later, and had come here to learn from him. He returned here as often as he could to assist Mr. Quiroga and to extend his own knowledge.

Basil's eyes were striking: something between bluish green and greenish brown, depending on the light. He had a strong, wide nose. He would close his mouth very firmly sometimes (Karolina imagined that his mother closed her mouth in much the same way). He showed her the scars on his shoulder and chest where the bullets had entered.

By the age of twelve she had already acquired a great deal of knowledge. At fourteen she entered a new phase—overnight, or within the space of a few months, she started out on the perilous road to mature womanhood. When years later she came round to committing her energies undividedly to the twenty-nine orders again, she had lost the innocent trustfulness she had brought to it before. Her renewed embrace of learning was no longer marked by a sense of wholeness.

WHEN SHE AND Basil got back to the hotel from the veld on Tuesday morning, a man and a woman were poring over a map on the stoep. When Karolina and Basil sat down at a table near them they looked up, and after a few minutes the woman addressed them in English. They needed some help, they were not sure of the route. Would they care to join them for a drink?

The woman was called Adelia Farber, the man Fernes Ramírez. They were touring the country. When she was a child she had come here often to visit her grandfather on his farm, but now she no longer recognised anything—she gestured towards a map—it was so long ago. "This is a nostalgic visit," she said, "I wanted my husband to get a sense of the country. He is not from these parts."

It was obvious that Fernes was not from these parts. Everything about him, from his name down to the tips of his exotic sandals, was not from these parts.

Adelia had a warm and passionate, but ironic face, her skin was extraordinarily pale, her hair heavy, her features Spanish. She wore pearls.

Fernes had eyes like gemstones. His skin and hair colouring were unusual—a high skin colour, like a flush of blood to the face (even to the scalp); jet-black hair like a raven's wing, cropped short in front, but with a long, seductive lock in the nape of his neck. He was clean-shaven, but with the shadow of a bluish black beard, and he seemed extremely restless.

As they pored over the road maps together, Adelia told them that her mother was Spanish and her father South African. She had spent part of her early childhood in South Africa, before her family had moved to South America. Fernes had an American mother and a Chilean father. He was born in South America, but he was educated mainly in the United States. They lived in Bogotá, Colombia, now. Adelia was a painter, Fernes an art dealer, Karolina gathered. This was his first visit to South Africa, Adelia had brought him here to show him the land of her birth.

They explained that their recent trip to Italy had been completely ruined by a crazy Italian friend of Fernes's. The friend had taken them under his wing, and would not allow them to go where they had intended—to Siena, to Padua, to Venice, to see the divine frescoes of Veronese, to see Giotto and Piero della Francesca. No, the man had said, they had better come to his villa in the country. It would be much better to gain an intimate knowledge of one particular part of the country than to rush around like tourists, like vulgar *turisti*. The farmhouse turned out to be an absolute ruin—not nearly what they had been led to expect, with nothing in sight but a few miserable olive trees. Adelia promptly contracted bronchitis. The friend took them to a nearby spa (so-called)—an abandoned tannery at the edge of a shallow dam. Its water came from a distant hot-water spa, brought in by means of a channel, its curative properties long dispersed. They lay in the blackish green, slimy water and stared at the murky sky. The crazy Italian and his mistress swam (Fernes imitated his slow, laborious, doglike crawl through the water, eyes wide open, wearing a swimming cap). The man asked Adelia (in broken English) if she had ever wanted to make fuck with a black man, he asked if she had ever wanted to make fuck with two men at the same time. No, Adelia replied. How bourgeois, the man said. They all lay in the shallow, brownish green, slimy, lukewarm water by the tannery, like frogs in a shallow pond. They looked up listlessly at the warm, brooding sky. While they were folding bedsheets in the laundry the following day, the man asked Adelia to marry him. He then took them to a nearby lake where the pope sometimes came to bathe (very occasionally). They made a laborious descent down the steep, pine-covered slopes, cutting their feet on the loose stones. Upon reaching the lake, the friend stripped down and jumped into the water, whereupon his small son, who had accompanied them, promptly experienced an Oedipal crisis. Daddy, Daddy, he cried, why do you show them your *piccolino*? The child screamed, splashed them with water, and hurled stones at them. Why should I be exposed to this child's Oedipal fears right now, here, at this particular moment in my life? Adelia thought. The man rose up from the water, streams of water running down his body, overgrown with dense black fur, and said in his heavy Italian accent (which Fernes imitated exceedingly well): how strange that the child should be so protective of his *piccolino*. Very strange, Adelia remarked dryly, staring straight ahead. She spent the next three weeks recovering from bronchitis, and they never saw the divine blues and pinks and golds of Paolo Veronese. This had happened immediately before they left for Africa.

Karolina was unaccountably drawn to Adelia from the moment they met. She listened to her in wonderment, from time to time looking up at the Free State sky, at the Southern African sky above them—vast, unending, cloudless.

"Do you know Judith Pohl?" she asked Adelia after a moment's hesitation. "Have you ever met her here, or elsewhere?"

"No," said Adelia. "Should I know her?"

"No," said Karolina. "I don't know why I thought you may have met her somewhere. She left this country a long time ago. I've lost touch with her, actually."

When they had sufficiently orientated themselves in regard to the road maps, the couple took leave of them. They promised to call here again on their return journey and disappeared over the northern horizon in a column of dust, into the same nothingness they had so unexpectedly come out of.

THAT NIGHT Karolina took a parcel containing the few letters that had escaped the fire from her travelling bag on top of the wardrobe, and read again the letter that Judith Pohl had written to her more than fifteen years ago.

Again she was struck by a single line: "Some day I shall astound you, and I shall be able to speak to you of something—my revelation."

Some day I shall astound you.

CHAPTER 9

NIGHTS OF reckless passion now followed for Karolina Ferreira and Jess Jankowitz.

The moon rose and the moon went down. The moon described a perfect semicircle reaching from one end of the horizon to the other. Karolina found that not even its cool light could dull the glow of this man.

She breathed easily, like someone who lived with no effort at all.

"The present moment. This moment. Where I am now," Jess said, "this is where I want to be. Fulfilment no longer lies elsewhere, like before."

Karolina lay in his arm; she heeded his words. Now and then she would study the open palm of her hand by the light of the moon.

IN TOWN ON Wednesday afternoon, as Karolina was on her way to the post office, walking down the right-hand side of the main street in the cool shade of the shop front verandahs, a man came out of Pep Stores as if in a dream. She recognised him immediately. It was the man who had come out of his house in the township. His name was Philemon Mhlambi—she had recently clipped a small report on him from the local newspaper. It stated briefly that he worked in town, and that his entire family had been murdered in a violent incident. Karolina was alarmed by the expression on his face.

Around the corner Kieliemann was keeping a close watch on her from behind a pillar. He had his hand on the walkie-talkie at his hip, close to his fly, where the blue trousers appeared to be somewhat strained.

Karolina was so perturbed by the appearance of Philemon Mhlambi that she forgot she had been on her way to the post office. Crossing the street at an angle, she entered the cool Village Pharmacy on the other side. The wooden floor with its worn floral wall-to-wall carpet seemed unusually springy beneath her feet today, she tested it as if trying to pick up a certain rhythm from it. She did so quite unconsciously. Today the chemist's shop unexpectedly reminded her of another space - the boarded up secondhand furniture store in Wakkerspruit, with the abandoned bride in the window.

She and Basil had arranged to have a drink in the ladies' bar after dinner. Karolina arrived early. The magistrate and Pol were not there yet. She sat down at the bar counter. She had never been here with Jess; they did not play snooker together. She ordered a whisky. Since it was the middle of the week, there were only a few people there; in the snooker room next door she could hear the sound of Kieliemann's voice.

Basil came in. There was a freshly groomed look about him and he rubbed his hands in a way that was more enthusiastic, less unemphatic than usual.

"I'm going to see my girlfriend," he said. "She'll be in Kroonstad this weekend for a conference."

Karolina felt a slight pang at the thought of Basil in the arms of a woman. (Now that the possibility presented itself so concretely for the first time.) She resented the thought of someone caressing the places where the bullets had entered and left. In the veld she and Basil were connected with no need for words. They were like two innocents, she thought, innocent in the way children or idiots are. Despite their considerable combined knowledge, they moved through the veld every day like two people who were ignorant of the world and its motives. (Even though the world seldom managed to surprise Basil.)

But tonight was different. They lowered their gaze before each other tonight as they had not done before. Karolina averted her eyes from his scars. One of these was barely visible—immediately to the right of the base of his throat, below the collarbone. As if his sexuality were acutely concentrated in this exact spot. A scar that had to be caressed with the tongue.

She wanted to place her left arm over her two breasts, and her right hand between her legs, so as to conceal her own three fiery spots from him. And her two fingers before the entrance to her mouth—as before a small chapel.

SHE WAS WOKEN up in her room during the night by a commotion outside and by the flashing yellow light of a police car on her ceiling. She had been in the middle of a dream in which a close friend appeared. The woman had let her down, preferred someone else's friendship over hers.

Karolina must have been in a deep sleep, she woke up not knowing where she was, confused by the urgent voices and flashing light outside. She dressed quickly and went downstairs.

A black man was talking, surrounded by a small number of black bystanders, as well as by Kieliemann and some other members of the force—in supportive or subversive capacity—it was not immediately apparent which it might be. Karolina made sure that Gert Els was not on the scene.

The man sat on the opened-out back flap of the police vehicle. He was covered with a blanket that was wrapped tightly around his shoulders. He seemed to be wearing nothing underneath it but a vest and a pair of trousers. Even though it was a warm night, his teeth were chattering, which made it difficult for him to speak coherently. He had been given a warm drink, for now and again he swallowed some liquid from the cap of a flask. Two black women stood a little apart from the rest, one draped in a blanket, occasionally weeping quietly into a corner of it. Kieliemann spoke for the police. Although he seemed impatient, he was allowing the man to tell his story without interruption. The scene resembled a photograph—the action frozen, white and black equally stark in the unnatural yellow light.

Karolina stood at some distance, making sure that Kieliemann did not see her. The yellow light penetrated everywhere, eclipsing even the bountiful light of the night sky, etching the scene in hellish desolation.

The man spoke coherently in spite of his shivering. His Afrikaans was fluent and he seldom interrupted himself. He kept his eyes fixed firmly on a point somewhere ahead of him as he spoke. Now and then he lifted his gaze and stared into the distance with an expression as if he too had recently had some sort of revelation, like Philemon Mhlambi.

He had only just left Standerton, he said. (His face seemed somewhat out of focus in this light.) He and his brother were stopped at approximately two o'clock this afternoon by five men who demanded to know where they lived. They had fled one of the hostels in the area two days ago, after they had been harassed for being members of Numsa. So they gave someone else's address as their own.

The five men then held them at gunpoint, searched them, and took them to another hostel some distance away. They tied their hands behind their backs with wire and for three hours interrogated them about their affiliations.

When they stated their support for Ndamase, their captors told them that they were going to kill them for not supporting Sotsu. They begged for mercy, they said that Ndamase was not a thug, they pointed out to these people that the two factions had agreed to work together for peace.

Another man came in. He ignored their pleas, repeating over and over that they would be killed today. The men despatched someone to the hostel to find out why the two of them had left there. When he came back after an hour he said the residents had told him that the pair had run away because they supported Ndamase—they should be killed. When his brother asked who the man had spoken to at the hostel, the others replied that they did not need to know because they were going to be killed.

Two more men joined the group, all of them armed. He and his brother were forced into a car and taken to the cemetery. They persuaded their captors to untie their hands before killing them. He managed to get away—in spite of the shots fired at him—and he hid in the bushes. When he returned to the cemetery later on, he found his brother's body there with a single bullet wound to the head. After that he immediately fled to this place.

This was the man's story. He would take the police there right now to show them, he said. But he would not go back there by himself.

"Well, you'd better come along then," said Kieliemann. "We'll take you to the police station for the night. We'll find out tomorrow what the police in Standerton have to say."

The man turned round without a word and got into the back of the police van. Karolina noticed two young men she had never seen in the snooker room, in reservist uniform. One of them seemed strangely familiar, but she could not place him straight away. Kieliemann shut the doors, walked round the front of the vehicle, and got in on the driver's side with Gert Visagie next to him. They pulled away at high speed, made a sharp U-turn, and drove down the street. All of a sudden Karolina remembered that the prison was at the lower end of town, to the left as one entered. How did she know this?

The black bystanders began to move off in the direction of the township. Only Karolina still remained in the street, momentarily indecisive before deciding to walk towards town, along Stiebeuel Street. It was half past two. She tapped softly at Jess's window.

He received her into his bed with urgency. His body was scorching hot.

Karolina did not say much. She wondered what sort of consolation the man had in his cell tonight. In the early hours of the morning she suddenly remembered where she had seen the young man in reservist uniform before. He was the injured man from whose leg blood had spurted so copiously.

CHAPTER 10

IN THE COURSE of her walks through town Karolina was constantly on the lookout for the lovers. As if she wanted their intimacy to mirror her own experience. Although it was somewhat of a detour, and extremely hot, she and Basil would walk back every afternoon along the road that ran past the cemetery. They did so at her request. This was where she had first seen the lovers together, and this was where she expected to find them again.

At the hotel she would peep swiftly into the lounge to see if the (gentlemanly) husband should be sitting motionlessly over an untouched beer—a sign that the woman was elsewhere, with the lover, with or without his knowledge.

There had been no sign of Beyers and Delarey and the rest of the players since the night Karolina saw them in the ladies' bar. Nor of the woman or her long-suffering husband.

KAROLINA FOUND the cemetery a remarkably beautiful place. There was a fence along the front, there were low hedges inside, separating the various sections. Between the graves the earth was a sandy, pinkish brown. In the farthermost section there were a large number of cypress-like trees, and two large cypresses in the older part at the very front—two beautiful trees, reaching upward from the soft, pebbly pink earth, in unison with the stone monuments. Far in the background, as far as the eye could see, were the tranquil, unaccentuated, brownish green hills. The surroundings were so open, so unmarred, the graves so peaceful within this wide context. There were monuments of pale and of dark marble, of granite, and of a soft pinkish brown stone that appeared to have come from the immediate surroundings. As the graves all faced in the opposite direction, away from the road, the inscriptions could not be read from where they were walking.

The cicadas shrilled, but beyond this sound there was a profound stillness. Karolina, all the while keeping a dreamy or a speculative eye on the graves as they were walking, asked Basil today to tell her again of his experience in Botswana.

They laid hands on him there at night. This caused his body to vibrate to a strange rhythm. He was sometimes unbearably hot during the day, like a larva in a cocoon. He had hallucinations in which, removed from his protective coverings, his flesh felt loose, boiled soft, as if it would easily fall away from his bones. As if he had been stewing away like food. He had terrors and nightmares in which his body was profoundly violated—in which he lost his teeth, his hair, his nails; his penis came away like a morsel of boneless meat, it rolled away from him like a useless object made of clay. His face caved in. Sores, wounds, cavities replaced his hair, eyes, nails. The leaves covering him were constantly metamorphosing—smooth surfaces grew rough, crinkled surfaces grew furry, turning into skin, into membrane. Inside and outside became indistinguishable. Was the mouth the thing on the inside or the thing on the outside? And the skin? The leaves? The cover? The reliability of his senses was profoundly—terrifyingly—impaired.

Basil explained the effect of being bitten by a Gabon viper. The victim is not killed by the poison, but by the shock sustained through the sudden introduction into the body of a large dose of poison. Similarly, in the case of a bullet wound, the shock is produced by the violent penetration of the body—the brutal violation of the integrity of the body—rather than by the actual injury.

ON FRIDAY NIGHT Karolina's breathing in Jess's bed was deep and regular. The whole world seemed to her in perfect equilibrium.

On Saturday night she danced as she had not danced before with the Kolyn fellow in the dining room under the six panels.

She brought a new erotic dimension to the dance tonight—ardent but restrained. The Kolyn fellow seemed perfectly unruffled, but he was sweating with the sheer effort of it, using all the dancing skills at his disposal to keep up with her, exerting himself to the utmost. Karolina subordinated her will to his, and he led and supported her to the best of his ability.

In time the other dancers began unobtrusively to watch the dancing couple. Before their incredulous eyes Karolina and the Kolyn fellow turned into a single flame. Their two separate wills melted into one. The transformation was complete. As the night and the dance progressed, as the music grew more compelling, as the stars increased in brilliance (grew crisper), as the night sky grew more velvety, so her thighs became suppler; so, as she leaned far back, her hair almost brushed the surface of the wooden floor.

So, an energy was generated within her body that rose up along the spinal column—from the coccyx to the top of her head—where the fontanelle had closed more than thirty-five years ago like the hatches of a submarine.

Until eventually her body sang like a long-distance telegraph wire and she pulsed from head to toe like a high frequency signal. Until the Kolyn fellow in his ignorance realised that something truly extraordinary was at hand.

The woman before him was being transformed, and he did not remain untouched by it. His own hidden powers were set free too.

As their combined energy field expanded, the other dancers moved away to clear a space for them, and from time to time the figures of Pol, Lieutenant Kieliemann, and the magistrate would appear in the doorway leading off the dining room to the ladies' bar and snooker room. Karolina was unaware of this—she had long since entered a plane of altered sensory awareness.

Pol's face was wet with perspiration, his head as sleek as an otter's. His expression was inscrutable, but he would shudder visibly every time he turned away. Kieliemann would turn away without a word, adjusting the taut blue Terylene bulge when unobserved, flexing his muscles back in the snooker room, and when it was his turn to shoot, he would take aim with his cue, tense but unseeing. The magistrate, once he was settled in his chair again, seemed to be committing something to memory for future use, sucking pensively at the rim of his glass, his cold eyes expressionless.

The coloured lights on the stoep stirred lightly in the breeze. Karolina and the Kolyn fellow danced until late. Surrounded by noise, by people drinking and playing in the hotel, by the yellow light of a police vehicle flashing on and off in the street outside, and by the incessant comings and goings in the rest of the hotel. While in the ladies' bar and in the snooker room—where one could go mad and lose one's head—the demise of souls was plotted and might even be brought about tonight.

Against this backdrop of intrigue and innocent Afrikaner jokes Karolina and the Kolyn fellow continued to dance until deep into the night.

KAROLINA LAY with her head in the hollow of Jess's shoulder, listening to the regular beating of his heart. They lay together in his room. She stroked his warm body, covered with bronze fur.

He spoke, she listened. Sometimes she spoke. She questioned him, he replied. He asked questions, she explained.

If he should meditate on his own suffering, there would not be that much to focus on, he said, his own suffering seemed a little insignificant. He laughed.

So far she had had little cause for complaint, and not much to rejoice at either, she told him. (She did not tell him about the woman's prediction.)

He was better off now than he had been for a very long time, he said. He no longer had the same painful need for gratification from elsewhere.

Karolina lay with her eyes open, listening. When she turned her head to the left, and looked up slightly, she saw a Tibetan tanka on the wall.

Jess explained the meaning of the image to her. It represented Yama, the lord of death, invisible against a black background of non-existence. He could be recognised by his ornaments and attributes only—moving energies in a black field. These energies were represented by a raging fire, by writhing snakes, by the stripes in the skin of a flayed tiger, by the whirling motions of storms, by a raging downpour and streaks of lightning, by a tree of fire. The invisible Yama carried a sword to cut away ignorance; he wore a garland of severed heads, and a crown consisting of the skulls of the five Dhyani Buddhas. Flayed human skins with dangling heads, eyes, feet and hands were depicted in the top part of the picture. A raging buffalo bull that Yama would sometimes ride was copulating with a human figure, at the same time trampling it underfoot. Two halved skulls on either side were filled with blood and white seed energy. The earth of this burial ground was strewn with fragments of bone and a tiny, terrified, adoring worshipper squatted in the lower left-hand corner. The colours were blue, red and white on a black background.

This was the spiritual principle made visible, Jess explained, and the painting was charged with its energy, the energy of death.

When Karolina turned her head to the right, she imagined she could hear the faint rustle of insect feet on the leaves outside.

The hosts of the six kingdoms! And of the twenty-nine orders!

CHAPTER 11

ADELIA FARBER and Fernes Ramirez had promised to go on a picnic with Karolina and Basil when they returned, but could not say when that would be. They were still touring the country. Adelia told them that she had been in a serious car accident a year ago, from which she had not yet fully recovered. (Karolina had noticed that her movements were stiff, somewhat laboured. She hoped to see Adelia and Fernes again, because she had been so unaccountably affected by Adelia, and because behind her, her (dear, lost) friend Judith Pohl had unexpectedly risen up. It was not that Karolina saw an obvious similarity between the two women—the association had simply been there from the very beginning.

AFTER THE NIGHT of the incident outside the hotel, when the black man had told of his escape in the flashing yellow light of the police vehicle, Karolina decided to move out. Having seen the hotel flooded by that hellish, desolate light, she no longer wished to stay there. And she could hardly afford to do so by now.

She left the hotel at the end of the eighth week of her stay in Voorspoed, moved into a room in a large old house owned by a widow, situated at the corner of Water and Sluis Streets. The house was approximately halfway between the hotel and the house where

Jess lodged. She did not intend cutting her ties with the hotel. She would continue to go there to play snooker and to dance, and to eat in the dining room so she could look at the painted panels.

She had already remained in this town longer than she had intended, but her field work was not yet completed, and she had no desire to return to the city just yet. Her life there seemed increasingly insubstantial and unappealing.

She had lain on her bed in the city and she had stared through her window at the oppressive grey sky and the raging vegetation. She had wondered whether she would have to remain lying there like that for the rest of her life, contemplating waste and ruin.

ON SUNDAY AFTERNOON Karolina and Jess had lunch together at the Rendezvous Café. The menu offered a choice of Vrystaat Steak (rump steak), Boere Vrystaat Steak (T-bone), a Transvaler Grill (with traditional boerewors), a Nataller Grill (with mutton chops), a Kapenaar (with fish), a Honolulu Barbecue (served with tinned pineapple), a Medium Lunch, and a Mixed Grill. The tomato sauce dispenser was in the shape of a tomato. Against one wall was a poster depicting a Scandinavian mountain stream with rocks, birches and pines, and on the wooden divider a garish print of flamenco dancers.

"Repos ailleurs," said Jess.

They sat down at the table nearest the rear window, next to two huge freezers with soiled covers. Today they were not reflected in the mirror.

"I have no regrets," Jess said. He spoke of the dreams he had had. The dream of a hedonistic life, of a life of perfect harmony. The dream of perfect union with a woman. Dreams of a world without shadows!

When they had eaten, they crossed the hot, still town to his room with its cream curtains.

While Karolina turned silent in his embrace, only then did Jess become truly articulate. His reserve made way for an inspired deluge—ardent exclamations of tenderness, wonderment and incredulity.

She was grateful for the profusion of it all.

TIME STOOD STILL when they were in each other's arms. It must seem so to all lovers, Karolina thought. Gert Els, Kieliemann, Pol, the magistrate, all of them ceased to exist, and so did the veld, the hotel, the snooker room, the drought, the reps, the travellers. Basil was not on his way to meet his beloved, his heart filled with desire.

BASIL RETURNED from his amorous sojourn in Kroonstad on Wednesday evening, and he and Karolina had a drink in the ladies' bar. They were slightly embarrassed in each other's company at first. Karolina was reluctant to enquire about the meeting with his beloved—she both wanted and did not want to know.

Tonnie de Melck was sitting at the counter a few places further down, a redheaded woman at his side—the one Karolina had seen him with on the night of the performance. His wife, presumably.

She did not want to stare openly, but Karolina was most captivated by the couple. The woman had short, red hair, cut in a style that was most certainly not seen in these parts very often. It was of a shade remarkably similar to the deep red feathers of a Rhode Island Red rooster; the way it fell over her forehead unmistakably suggested the fringe of a Rhesus monkey. This hairstyle was so cryptic, so obscure, so difficult to decipher, that Karolina found it virtually impossible to grasp the logic of it at a single sitting. There was a multifacetedness about the style, a suggestion of multiple viewpoints, that did not allow for immediate synthesis on the part of the spectator. This hairstyle was possibly stranger than anything ever seen on this side of the Brandwater Basin. It was a creation that could only have been dreamed up in a large metropolis.

Her clothes, too, would probably send a delicious, forbidden, collective shiver of disapproval and of grudging admiration through onlookers in the streets of this town. She wore a very short dress in a soft floral print, and black men's shoes with matching black school socks. Her calves were shapely, like those of a dancer or a gymnast.

But her eyes were probably her most striking feature. They were the palest eyes Karolina had ever seen in a human being. If they were one shade paler, they would be completely colourless. They looked like eyes of glass—the glassy blue of certain marbles. Not a beautiful woman, but the kind of woman men might come to blows about, Karolina thought.

The woman drank in a detached sort of way. She seemed self-conscious and absent at the same time. There was no conversation between her and her husband. His blondness seemed somewhat toned down tonight.

The room filled up gradually. The magistrate (hands unsoiled) sat in his corner, sucking at the rim of his glass. Pol came in too. Karolina sensed his humid presence even before he came up close and touched her arm.

She turned round, pleased to see him. (Seeing him always made her feel happy.)

To begin with, he merely smiled from ear to ear—an oiled, smooth smile, a striking predominance of horizontal lines on his perspiring face.

He gave her arm a small, firm squeeze, brought his wet, warm head closer to hers.

"How are you?" he asked significantly. (Even a question as innocent as this was loaded with suggestion.)

"I'm well," she said.

He drew his head back again, gave her a deep, searching look. "'No one to pine/ as they dance and dine/ forsaken and forlorn am I,'" he quoted.

"Do you have a message for me?" she asked.

He shuddered lightly. Looked round the room furtively. Allowed his gaze to linger on the redheaded wife. Shuddered again.

"Why would we have brought this beautiful temptress here tonight?" he asked softly, in conspiratorial tones. "This lad does not know the end of his riches or his sorrows," he added, inclining his head slightly towards Tonnie de Melck.

They both gazed covertly at the drinking couple. Karolina saw Tonnie sitting with both elbows on the bar counter, his head drawn into his shoulders.

"What's happening in town?" Karolina asked Pol.

"The usual shit," he said, fixing his long, fond, watery gaze on her. "One is tempted to see the hand of God in all of this." With these words he took leave of her, and returned to his circle of friends in the corner.

Before long he started up his first song of the evening, his favourite song: "When I Was a Mere Schoolboy."

SOON AFTERWARDS Karolina and Basil left the ladies' bar to play a few rounds of snooker. They sat together as usual on the cane seat under the horned kudu head and the beer poster.

"That man is not happy," Basil suddenly remarked, even before Karolina could ask him about Tonnie de Melck. "His depression is characterised by despair, it grows worse at night and when he's drinking. His moods tend to fluctuate, he is critical of himself. The future seems very dark to him. He's the kind of man who would never threaten suicide—he'd simply do it."

"Then his wife is probably not an ideal companion for him," said Karolina.

Basil chewed on a matchstick. "No," he said. For a while he sat staring before him absentmindedly.

"What is it you're thinking now?" asked Karolina. "You seem upset."

Basil hesitated. "Things don't look too good for him," he said.

"What is it you're thinking?" asked Karolina. "Will he do something?"

But Basil merely shrugged, he would say nothing more.

CHAPTER 12

KAROLINA DID not go into the veld with Basil the day after she had received a letter, out of the blue and unheralded, from her only sister. The letter could hardly have come from a more remote place: Victoria Island in the Beaufort Sea.

Towards the end of the morning she walked aimlessly through the centre of town. She was both thrilled and distressed, filled with a vivid sense of her sister's presence, called forth so unexpectedly by her letter.

It had reached her in a roundabout way, via her city address. There it was, the previous afternoon, in the widow's entrance hall, and all of a sudden all three of them were with her—her mother, her father, and her sister.

Not many whites were out on the streets at this time of day. The wide main street was quiet. The town had a low vertical profile, no more than a few double-storeyed buildings—it was flat and sprawling, the most prominent landmark being the church steeple at the southern end, flanked by two tall Christmas pines.

Again and again she was surprised at how little the town had changed over the past twenty-five years, how little had been altered. The wide cement stoeps outside the shops were the same, and the verandahs supported by cast-iron posts or concrete pillars. The spacious shops with high, ornate ceilings, wooden floors and deep windowsills had remained unchanged. Much had been preserved, the facades of some buildings probably dated back to the founding of the town.

She walked aimlessly through the town, past small groups of black schoolchildren, past unemployed young people, women on bicycles coming into town from the farms, stately older women, mothers with young children and infants who sat in the symmetrical, circular patches of shade cast by two small trees, pruned into spheres, at the entrance to the post office.

There was a lump of longing in her throat as she walked.

SHE HAD NOT been in time to be at her father's side as he was dying. She had received an urgent message, but when she arrived at the hospital (having spent a day travelling there), he had already died.

The nurse had left her alone with him. She had turned back the sheet to see his face. Then she had taken his cold hand and placed it in hers.

WHILE SHE WAS waiting for Basil to join her for lunch, she had a cold drink on the hotel stoep. Where the town ended, the surrounding brown, grass-covered hills were visible. Today the cloud formations all inclined to the right. A few small clouds (the size of a man's hand) immediately above the horizon, above them some heavier formations, and then the infinite, open, blue sky. Did anybody still bother about the clouds? The daily formations had long since ceased to yield anything.

She read her sister's letter again. It was not long—her sister had never been a person of many words. She stated where she was (the same cold, remote corner of the world), what she was working on (the mineral kingdom, still). She asked how Karolina was doing. The letter was little more than a long-distance signal.

She saw Basil approaching from a distance, and she was pleased to see him. As they entered the hotel, she peeped briefly into the lounge, as usual. The husband was sitting in a corner over an untouched beer, his broad, long-suffering back turned to them.

"Jurie Beyers is in town," Karolina said to Basil immediately. "He must be with the wife right now."

"I saw them this morning," said Basil.

"Where?" asked Karolina.

"In the veld," said Basil.

"Damn," she said, "why didn't I go along?"

She studied the gentle, cosmic explosions in the Battle of Majuba high up on the wall of the dining room. The sky was filled with signs for those who cared to pay attention. The human aspect was diminished, scaled down—it was the landscape that was heroic, that triumphed, not the two insignificant fighting parties.

When one meditates on death, there are two things that should be kept in mind, Jess had said. One is the fact that one will certainly die, and the other that one does not know the time and circumstances of one's death.

Doesn't this make you feel panicky? she had asked.

No, he had said. One learns to accept it. The more one concentrates on the fact of death, the more profound one's sense of the ephemeral nature of human existence.

Do you believe this? Have you experienced this? she had asked.

Looking at the panels, Karolina today saw that this was indeed so—life is transitory, fragile; human activity is insignificant, virtually without historical substance. (More difficult to see it this way while lying in Jess's arms!)

Basil, usually so controlled, was agitated today. There seemed to be few things that could really upset him, but today he was on edge. He crumbled the bread between his fingers nervously, he played with the fork; every so often he would even look over his shoulder apprehensively.

"What's the matter, Basil?" asked Karolina.

Basil chewed on a toothpick. Shook his head.

"Have you seen something? Something concerning Beyers and Delarey? Something concerning the lovers?" she asked.

Basil sighed. She looked into his eyes. It almost seemed as if he were asking something of her.

"Shall we play a game or two tomorrow night?" she asked.

Basil nodded, then rose all of a sudden, as if determined to leave his restless mood behind right there. As they were leaving, it occurred to her that one possibility she had not considered or raised was that the recent separation from the woman he loved might be hard for him to bear.

ON FRIDAY NIGHT there was a tumultuous noise in the ladies' bar from early on. Pol was there, the magistrate was there. There were more players than usual in the snooker room. Among them were Kieliemann, Yap Buytendach, Boet Visagie, the two FAK individuals (minus pullovers), Balls Baluschagne and the two other teachers (Abel Kriek and the Latin master, Tiny Botha), Doctor Manie Maritz, a few reps, a few salesmen, as well as Tonnie de Melck and some of the local farmers.

Yap, Balls, and the pair of teachers sat in the green and maroon imitation leather easy chairs against the wall to the right, under the antelope heads and the beer posters. The farmers and the reps sat at a small, low, round table next to theirs, under the framed photographs of stud bulls (prize-winning entries in the local agricultural shows of the past few years). Karolina and Basil sat in their customary place—on the cane seat to the right of the door leading to the ladies' bar, under the kudu head.

Karolina drank whisky and observed the others. There was something unusual about Tonnie de Melck tonight. His face was flushed, as if from a great rush of blood to his head. His hair positively shone under the light, it set him apart from the others. He smoked incessantly, hardly spoke, his face strangely expressionless.

Basil participated actively in the game tonight, it seemed he was unable to keep still; he also drank more than usual. Karolina reacted to his restlessness—she drank more too. The room seemed smaller, the walls more intensely yellow, the light shining down on the green surface of the table more concentrated. The atmosphere was more impenetrable, more densely filled with smoke, with laughter and with talk.

Initially there was the usual male talk—the hand on the cock talk, the discussions of bloodlines and sperm counts, pesticides and pistols, cars and farm implements, sports results and statistics, livestock sales and diseases affecting the maize.

But gradually the murky contents broke away from their dark matrix and rose to the surface, dislodged by the liquor, the tumult, and the incessant talk. In time the insinuations became darker, the jokes less coherent, the lure of danger more enticing.

Karolina was startled when Tonnie de Melck unexpectedly jumped up from his chair and left hurriedly through the back door. Those remaining behind at his table stared after him, as did Basil, whose expression was hard to define.

"Why the hell is De Melck rushing off like a lunatic?" asked Boet Visagie.

"Maybe he's gone to knock some sense into his wife," said Kieliemann. There was laughter.

They carried on playing. Those who did not play snooker, carried on drinking. Everyone talked. The room was thick with smoke and with the heat generated by the players. Karolina wondered if the wife with the red mane might indeed be a problem to Tonnie de Melck. Things looked bad for him, Basil had said, and Pol had said that he was burdened with cares. She drank whisky, she observed the players—by now she knew the various expressions of concentration as they leant forward to sink the ball (the portraits of the pair of Free State snooker champions on the wall facing the snooker table watching over them with intimidating authority).

The night wore on. The laughter grew more uproarious, the conversations frayed, the subterranean psychic wiring was increasingly laid bare.

After some time Karolina paid a brief visit to the ladies' bar. She was hoping she might find Pol there and had barely seated herself on one of the little bar stools in the far right-hand corner when he came up to her.

By this time he, too, was considerably transformed, and his disintegration well advanced.

"Beyers and Delarey are in town," he said, coming straight to the point, his head inclined sharply towards her.

"What is the purpose of their visit?" she asked (delighted at the news).

Pol looked round the room, then replied, in tones lower than usual: "Those lads are having one hell of a go at organising the township this weekend."

"Why not stage another performance instead?" asked Karolina. She, too, was coming apart a little because of the whisky.

Pol gave a cunning smile.

"I shudder to think of everything these lads might stage for us yet," he said.

"What exactly might that be?" asked Karolina.

"The most gruesome tragedies," said Pol.

"Tell me now, once and for all, just what it is they have up their sleeves," said Karolina.

"These two lads are filled with the spirit of enterprise," said Pol. "But they better be careful, or they will be rapped on the knuckles before long."

"Are they not careful enough?" asked Karolina.

"Arrogance," said Pol. "Arrogance is Beyers's greatest weakness. He's somewhat like the young Sigmund Freud—there's nothing he won't take on."

"And the woman?" asked Karolina.

"Which one?" Pol asked darkly.

"The beautiful one. Is there more than one?"

Pol drew up his shoulders dramatically. Rolled his eyes towards the ceiling. Looked at Karolina long and feelingly before he replied: "As I say, there's nothing this lad won't take on. There's always room for another beloved."

(Karolina remembered the tenderness of Beyers's gaze as he looked upon the beautiful woman in the café.)

She took leave of Pol and returned to the snooker room, where the combined onslaught of alcohol and nicotine, the rising temperature of the room, the growing excitement of the game, the rousing talk (facilitating the increasingly rash intrusions on forbidden ground), had gradually brought about some subtle mental and bodily changes. There was a gradual shift in the workings of the sympathetic and the parasympathetic nervous system, as well as in the functioning of the voluntary and involuntary muscles. Skin temperature and secretions of sweat fluctuated, the heartbeat accelerated, the lungs expanded, the liver and the kidneys worked harder, the bladder filled up, blood sugar levels rose and fell more rapidly, the scrotum grew warmer, the penis shrank and cooled down.

Every variety of urine intermingled in the toilets. Sometimes it would be highly coloured, with a beerish odour, while at other times it would smell of horse feed, or of violets, or grass, or it might be acrid or offensive. Sometimes the spurt would be dark and profuse, sometimes it would be an angry drip, clear and copious, or forked, arched or angled. The colour varied from saffron yellow to straw yellow, from reddish brown to acid green, it was milky, red, opaque or clear, sometimes black and bloody, scalding hot or lukewarm, or warm as blood and foamy. So many coded messages—every single one of them wasted on all but the rare individual who had eyes to read and an ability to decipher it.

Basil had only just returned from the toilet when a number of things occurred in rapid succession.

Gert Els appeared in the doorway through which Basil had just entered the snooker room. The moment he entered, all activity in the room ceased for a few moments, and everyone looked in his direction.

He was taller by at least a head than most of the men in the room, and utterly devoid of colour—hair, eyes, skin were all one shade. But tonight his face was so extraordinarily pale, so deathly pale that there was a greenish-blue tinge to it. His gaze was cold and mistrustful, his jaw was clenched, there was sweat on his forehead. His eyelids seemed heavy and dry. The baton tapped restlessly but rhythmically against his thigh. Gert Els took stock of those present in the room and summoned Kieliemann, Buytendach and Visagie to his side with an almost imperceptible movement of his head.

From the corner of her eye (she sat motionless in order to remain as inconspicuous as possible) she observed how still Basil, too, sat beside her, and she noticed the motionless figure of Pol Habermaut hovering almost invisibly, glass in hand, in the doorway leading to the ladies' bar.

Then Gert Els and the three men departed (the others were probably waiting outside in the police vehicle), and once again the room filled up with smoke, with laughter, and with talk.

Karolina glanced surreptitiously at Basil sitting next to her, he did not seem very happy.

"Gert Els looks pretty shitty, doesn't he?" she said softly, without facing him directly.

Basil nodded in agreement. "Only the surface of his skin is cold," he said.

Shortly afterwards there was another interruption, the second of the evening. Jurie Beyers entered the snooker room through the same door Gert Els and his henchmen had left by a few minutes ago. There was a look of urgency about him, and his expression was tense. Like Gert Els before him, he surveyed the gathering briefly, pausing momentarily in the doorway, keeping his hand on the door handle all the while. Then he closed the door behind him softly, and passed noiselessly through the snooker room to the ladies' bar. As he passed Karolina and Basil—still sitting together motionlessly on the cane seat—Karolina saw him giving, practically imperceptibly, the barest possible indication of a greeting to Basil.

Basil turned his head away from her slightly as he followed Beyers with his eyes. Then he rose suddenly and walked over to the snooker table to play.

Karolina remained in her seat. Had Beyers just come from the township? If so, Gert Els had fortunately not managed to catch him there tonight. Perhaps Basil and Beyers were better acquainted than Basil was prepared to admit, she thought this had to be the case.

Karolina remained in her seat. Her legs felt a little weak, but her head was much clearer than earlier in the evening. She had had a fright, and so had Basil.

From where she was sitting she could not see much of what was happening in the ladies' bar. She got up to see if Beyers was still there. She sat down at the bar counter in the corner closest to the door. Jurie Beyers was sitting practically opposite her on the other side. To his left, and sitting right beside him, was Tonnie de Melck's wife. When had she arrived? She seemed to be doing the talking and Beyers the listening. He had his back half turned away from Karolina, his right elbow on the counter, the fingers of his right hand lightly supporting his head. The woman was wearing a low-cut black dress, and judging by the expanse of (crossed) knee that was visible above the counter, the dress was also very short. The large zebra skin was stretched open across the wall behind her, higher up and to the right of it was a wildebeest head. Karolina thought the zebra skin echoed something of the exotic starkness of the woman's appearance.

She looked over her shoulder to see if she could find Pol. She had not heard any singing from his corner for some time. But he was indeed still there, sitting on the green imitation leather chair, glass in hand, surrounded by his friends. When he caught Karolina's eye, he gave her a meaningful nod, as if to say: Did I not predict that all these things would come to pass in exactly this way? Lowering his eyes, he put a finger to his lips as if to signal utmost caution.

The magistrate sat in his usual corner in the most distant part of the room. He was neither sullen nor reserved tonight—quite the contrary. He appeared to be in high spirits, apparently churning out jokes and anecdotes. His high-pitched laughter sounded up at ever shorter intervals as he seemed to laugh at his own jokes.

The hellish din continued unabated in the snooker room to the right of her. There was playing and drinking, there was raucous cunt and prick talk—the atmosphere thick with male emanations.

Karolina felt nauseous. She got up, she wanted to tell Basil that she was going home. She came into the snooker room as the younger De Melck brother entered by the back door. Only rarely had he seemed so radiantly blond, though there was an expression of unbearable despair in his face. He lingered momentarily in the doorway, the room quieting down somewhat, then he passed rapidly through the snooker room and into the ladies' bar.

Karolina knew where he was heading. Basil also knew, where he stood frozen by the snooker table. There was an expression of revulsion and compassion on his face.

Karolina turned back to the ladies' bar. By this time Tonnie de Melck had taken hold of his wife's arm, and had dragged her off the bar stool. There was an absolute hush in the room. Beyers came between them in an attempt to stop him, but De Melck pushed him away violently. Beyers ended up halfway across the counter, but he was on his feet again in an instant, like a cat. The wife had silently pulled herself free, but De Melck got a firmer grip on her arm, and dragged her away. After their initial tussle, she offered no resistance. Everybody's eyes were on the pair—more particularly on the wife's legs in sheer black silk stockings. They left, not a single word having been spoken by either of them.

A car door slammed shut outside, and a car pulled away at speed. There was an uproar in the ladies' bar, there was excited talk.

"That's right," Karolina heard a male voice exclaim, "discipline her!" This was followed by general laughter.

Karolina's heart was beating rapidly and her legs were shaky. She sat down on the cane seat for a while in order to get a grip on herself. Basil was still standing at the snooker table. Once again she felt there was an inarticulate appeal in his expression. He carried on playing, but it seemed he was finding it hard to concentrate on the game.

After a while Karolina rose and went to the ladies' bar to order another whisky. Jurie Beyers was still seated in the same spot. He was not talking to anybody. He had both elbows on the bar counter before him. The fingers of both hands were placed over his mouth. He sat very still, very upright. He gazed intently before him. He appeared to be concentrating intensely. The drink on the counter before him remained untouched.

She did not look over her shoulder to see if Pol was still around, but before long she felt his steamy heat against her left arm. He was standing close behind her. She turned towards him. He said nothing. He stood there, glass in hand, fairly dripping with perspiration.

"What happens next?" she asked.

"Shit," he said. "Infernal shit." He shifted his gaze slightly, as if in contemplation of the pile of steaming shit that was rising before his mind's eye.

"I shudder to think of all the shit in the land tonight," he said, rocking to and fro emphatically.

"It's positively buzzing," he said.

"The poor man," she said.

"That lad is heavily burdened with cares," said Pol.

"And Beyers?" she asked, very low, and inclined her head as inconspicuously as possible towards the place where he was sitting, motionless and attentive.

"I shudder to think of everything that might be on that lad's agenda," said Pol. He looked portentously and deeply into her eyes.

"I'm going home now," she said, and after they had said goodbye, she got up for the second time that night to tell Basil that she was feeling nauseous and wanted to leave.

As she entered the snooker room, a fourth person made an unexpected appearance at the back door. It was Sergeant Frikkie Visser.

"There's been a hell of an accident," he announced, "a hell of an accident!"

Basil stood on the other side of the green surface of the table. Karolina could tell by the expression on his face that he already knew to whom it had happened, and that he had already resigned himself to it—but nevertheless dreaded hearing about it.

TONNIE DE MELCK was dead. First he shot at his wife, at his brother and at the black servant who was trying to restrain him, and then he shot himself in the stomach. He then got back into his car (a new Mercedes), drove off towards town at high speed, and smashed into the side of another car (both occupants injured) before driving straight into a clay embankment.

KAROLINA AND BASIL walked home slowly. The night had suddenly grown chilly. They walked along Stiebeuel Street, passing the Voorspoed Electric Roller Mills on the left. They heard light footsteps and low voices coming from the far end of the mill yard. They were just in time to see Manie Delarey and two black men walking to a car parked some way up the street, getting into it, and driving off. It was half past two in the morning.

"That was Manie Delarey," said Karolina.

"Yes," said Basil.

"They were organising the township people tonight," she said.

"Yes," said Basil.

That must be why Beyers had been at the hotel, she thought. To draw the attention away from Delarey.

There was a cool, gibbous moon high up in the sky.

"Tell me, Basil," said Karolina, "are you able to foresee someone's death?"

"There was a time when I wasn't so good at it," said Basil (they were walking, he kept his gaze fixed firmly on the road before him). "I taught myself to do it, see. When I nearly died, that's when. That's when I began to cultivate the ability."

They walked along in silence for a while.

"Now I don't want to any more," he said. "But I can't pretend I don't see these things."

"How long have you known that Tonnie de Melck would die today?"

"Ever since the day I saw the shape of his shadow, five days ago," Basil replied, matter-of-factly. "And Wednesday night, in the bar."

"Couldn't you have warned him?"

"No," said Basil.

At the corner of Sluis and Water Streets they parted. Karolina did not even consider going by Jess's place. She did not think her sense of icy desolation could be dispelled tonight.

She had a dream in which her father appeared in a most unlikely guise. That is to say, in a flippant mood, completely unlike him. He said things that were not true, he made curious pronouncements.

She reprimanded him. That's not true, she said, how can it be so? Then he changed, he told her that his heart was aching intensely. But this cannot be, she thought, it was her heart—her sister's heart—that was aching.

CHAPTER 13

ON TUESDAY AFTERNOON Basil and Karolina sat side by side in a pew at the back of the church, just as they always did on the cane seat in the snooker room. They were attending the memorial service for Tonnie de Melck. They had known him too, Karolina thought, intimately, since Basil had known things about him no one else knew.

The church was packed. They sat towards the back so as to remain as inconspicuous as possible, but although they drew some veiled, disapproving looks, the family in the front pews was the main attraction today. The mood was subdued but sultry, a restless anticipation that was hard to contain.

The pulpit was in a style identical to that of the baroque staircase and the reception area of the hotel, Karolina saw with a thrill of recognition. The same grand, extravagant flower and leaf motifs, the same swelling, rounded forms in dark oak (satin smooth beneath the palm of the hand). The architect or sculptor must have had extraordinary powers of imagination to have ventured into these baroque excesses in the midst of the stark severity of this sheep and maize region.

The expensive, dark coffin stood under the baroque pulpit. Hard to believe that Tonnie de Melck was lying in it. His radiance extinguished. How long had he walked around with the idea of killing himself?

The minister appeared on the pulpit. A dull, ash blond man, the younger of a pair of local preachers. Karolina knew who they were, since she had once or twice heard them being addressed in fawning tones by the salesladies in the chemist's shop.

He spread out his black-robed arms. He is too much the poet, Karolina thought as soon as he began, he won't last long in this place.

"We cry unto God in a language that is confused and filled with weeping," he began. "We are all of us in a state of degeneracy, brought about through the exercise of our own will."

There was absolute silence in the church.

Brought about through the exercise of our own will; Karolina took note of this.

"We find ourselves in a state of bitter, ravaging spiritual drought caused by our own obduracy and by our own actions," he said, pausing, allowing his words to sink in.

"But things may be so very different," he continued. "Things may be so very different for every single one of us. Things might have been so very different for this unhappy, departed brother of ours."

Now he was on thin ice, Karolina thought.

It was dead quiet in the church. Did everyone want to know just how things might have been different for Tonnie de Melck? If he had not had so much money? If he had not had the autistic, wayward redhead by his side? If they had not been childless? If he had not been the younger son? If his father had not had different expectations of him? If his mother had not suffered from depression for many years? If the country had not been hit by a drought? If a single one or perhaps even two of the coincidences that had shaped the aggregate of his life had been different, would things have turned out differently for him? Karolina wondered.

"Things might have been so very different for him if the bountiful rain of God's grace had fallen on his soul," said the minister. "He would have blossomed, whereas now he has withered away! He would have borne fruit, whereas now the tree has been prematurely felled.

"But God did not will it this way. It pleased the Lord not to lead this brother to his cool oasis so that he may drink and bear fruit. Therefore, let us not sit in judgement. Let us see the unfortunate course of this departed brother's life as an expression of God's wisdom and of his great plan. But let us learn from it. Let it be a lesson to us. Let us cast off everything that comes between God and us—our stubborn and self-seeking ways, our obstinacy and our arrogance—so we may be open to God's grace when it should please Him to bestow it on us. Let us examine every corner of our own sinful hearts, let us say yes to God's glorious bounty.

"We are all of us dying creatures," said the minister, "yet the seeds of living hope are buried deep within us. Only by the grace of God shall we germinate and live!"

Karolina saw Pol sitting three rows ahead. He turned round once or twice, caught her eye complicitly before he turned his heavy, perspiring head away again. (Was he sitting there with a glass in his hand?)

She could also see the two FAK individuals, the two teachers—in front of and somewhat to the right of her—and Kieliemann, Boet Visagie, Frikkie Visser and Yap Buytendach to the left. The manageress of the hotel, the chemist's shop assistants, the owner of the Rendezvous Café, the owner of the Springbok Café, Steyn of Steyn and Sons Stationery, everyone was there, the entire town. And behind Karolina and Basil, in the very last row, the black domestic servants. One of them was sobbing quietly all the time.

"Break into our closed, rebellious hearts!" the minister prayed. "Into our hearts that have grown weak through sin. Let the bounty of early spring come gently into our unyielding hearts. This we pray with hankering, in anticipation of thy untold munificence. Let the bountiful rain of thy grace come down on us, even as it was withheld from our departed brother. From this brother who knew only thy drought, who never knew thy abundance. Behold us, Lord! Our lack of understanding! Our wilfulness! Our self-seeking ways! Behold us, but do not overlook our sins! Flagellate us! Do not spare us! Bend us to thy will—break us with thy plough that we may lie open like sun-scorched clods, ready to receive the abundant seeds of thy mercy!"

Karolina sat with head bowed. Basil sat motionless beside her. She dared not look at him.

Everyone remained seated after the service until the next of kin—gloriously made public in their grief and humiliation—had left the church, the eyes of the entire flock fixed scorchingly upon them. The patriarch (stout, authoritarian, dark blond) and the matriarch (a greyish blond woman, who must once have been a great beauty), the remaining brother (his arm in a sling), the sister-in-law, a single dissipated grandmother, male and female cousins, and the wife dressed in black. The singular cut of her dark red hair seemed even more outrageous in the sacred atmosphere of the church than it would in the streets of the town. She was pale as wax, but without expression, her face showed as little emotion as when Tonnie had dragged her away from the bar counter.

When they left the church the daylight was blinding. Karolina half stumbled. Basil steadied her. Someone touched her other arm lightly. It was Pol. The three of them proceeded silently along the gravel walk, heads bowed like professional mourners. Two huge Christmas firs and red roses in large round beds on either side of them. She had never seen Pol by daylight before.

"What exactly did the minister mean?" Karolina asked Pol in an undertone, once her eyes had become accustomed to the fierce daylight.

"Personally, I have absolutely no desire right now to go into that lad's own, inalienable insights," said Pol, speaking from the corner of his mouth.

He squinted up at the sun, gave her arm a little squeeze.

"But I shudder to think of those sunscorched clods," he said.

Karolina and Basil did not attend the interment. She would go to see the grave later, the next time she went past the cemetery, Karolina thought, as she walked home slowly in the heat with Basil.

AFTER THIS, Karolina drew back slightly from Jess's embrace. Tonnie de Melck's death had filled her mind with darkness. Darkness and doubt.

Jess must have picked up her mood, because he seemed downcast too.

"What's wrong?" he asked, but she was unable to reply.

She spent more time alone in her room in the widow's house in the afternoons. She would lie on her bed and dream, as she had done when she stayed at the hotel. It was early March, the late summer heat seemed to be abating gradually.

It was a pleasant room, she liked it there. There was a giant palm tree outside her window, but set against the open, clear blue sky, it seemed different from the palms in the city. The garden was beautiful. Outside her window were red cannas and pink stocks, scented flowers and fine, fragrant lawn, and a great variety of birds that sang all day long.

She would turn everything over and over in her mind. Many things had happened. Gert Els had not visited her in fantasy since she had left the hotel. Perhaps her relationship with Jess made her less permeable. Perhaps it was laying claim to all her fantasies—her mind less free to move where it wanted. She was no longer in dreamy contact with everyone. Love tied her down and burdened her, it beset her in a new way, it invaded her, she was like a city under siege. Was the bitter intensity of fleeting erotic pleasure enough to justify this? Had she not been better off when she had arrived here? Had she allowed herself to be misled by ridiculous predictions of eternal love and friendship?

The fate of the lovers no longer engaged her to the same extent—they could go their own sweet way for all she cared. If the beautiful woman should be blinded by love, if it should take possession of her and annihilate her—that was her own choice! If Jurie Beyers wanted to declare his love and commit himself in a thousand and one extravagant ways, he need spare no effort—he could shout it from the rooftops and from the stage, in cafés and in cemeteries, in uncountable shapes, disguises, and artificial colour changes (chameleon that he was). It was their life, it was their love, to do with and to go about as they pleased.

SHE RECEIVED a second letter in the post. (Having had no contact with anyone since she had come here.) It was a letter from Adelia Farber, with photographs of some of her paintings.

She described the places they had visited. She wrote that she found the country brutal, but exciting. They would continue to travel northwards for some distance before returning. The promise of lush vegetation to the east and to the north was irresistible, she said. She had this unending hunger after new landscapes. She mentioned that she and Fernes had been unwell, that Fernes felt acute anxiety at the sight of vast, open spaces, but that they managed to keep up their spirits as may be expected of exemplary travellers through Southern Africa.

In her paintings she was trying to portray herself as a hero, but it seemed it was not easy for women to be heroes, she said. One could not portray a woman in the heroic style in the same way as one could a man. Anything experienced by a man—however deviant—is immediately regarded as an extension of human experience, whereas the experience of a woman remained deviant, eccentric, idiosyncratic.

Karolina looked at the pictures and her scalp tightened at the sight of this woman's extraordinary vision. It shocked and unsettled her, yet gave her considerable pleasure.

THERE WAS A painting of a woman in a coffin in a vast, open plain, with a city in the background. She was wearing an elaborately embroidered shroud, depicting scenes from her life.

There was a self-portrait with an elaborate headdress of plaited rope and a beaded necklace. On her shoulder a crow was perched and in her hand she held a skull.

There was a self-portrait with strelitzias and giant, sensual leaves unfurling in the background.

There was a portrait of a woman with bare breasts, standing in front of an easel, a paintbrush in one hand, a palette in the other. Her gaze was open, confident, challenging. The large easel was half turned, its back towards the spectator, its contents obscured.

There were marvellous still lifes. A pawpaw that had been cut in half and that resembled female genitals; bananas, owls, and avocado pears; pineapples with leaves that were furled and twisted as in a vision. Moths, flayed hares, butterflies, coconuts, and words—letters bearing cryptic messages, sheet music, open books. There was a vanitas still life, with a burnished copper bowl, overripe fruit, dark roses, snails and a small, hidden snake.

There was a self-portrait where the organs inside her body, the pulsating heart, the blue innards, the female organs were as visible to the naked eye as her hair and her limbs.

There was a self-portrait of Adelia in a nun's habit. She sat in a chair with a pair of scissors in her hand, and all around her on the floor lay the luxuriant hair she had cut. These wisps of hair resembled flagella made of twine, instruments of torture; they were all over the bare surface of the floor, they were draped over the rails of the chair, they fell in a heavy, dark, fibrous plait over her knee.

The self-portraits were all done in three-quarter view, the torso in a frontal pose, the head turned slightly to the left; Adelia's proud, sensual face turned fixedly to the spectator.

Karolina studied these and thought, whatever Adelia may say, they doubtlessly were heroic portraits.

KAROLINA FELT it was time to go dancing again on Saturday night, to exorcise Tonnie de Melck's death.

She had felt the seductive rhythm rising up in her calves for some days now. She warmed up on top of the bed first, as she had done in the hotel. Here too, in the house of the widow, the creaking floorboards were far too noisy. She tried out the bed and found it sufficiently resilient.

Her hair was tied back tightly and she was dripping with perspiration. She recalled a conversation she had had with Jess. He had told her that the first noble truth of Buddhist teaching is that life is suffering. What caused this suffering? she had asked. The grasping ego, he had said.

She took a shower, painted her toenails, put on the red dress. She wondered how the young widow was doing—four days had passed since the funeral of Tonnie de Melck.

She thought of the dead man. His suffering had been so great that he had been compelled to put an end to it, but had his ego been that much more grasping than that of other people? Had he pushed God away through his obduracy and stubbornness, or had it pleased God to withhold his grace from him? Had his fate been irreversible, inevitable, or could his death have been prevented if someone (like Basil) had read the signs in his murky urine in time?

SHE DANCED with the Kolyn fellow. He wore the lace-up sneakers and short pants. His testicles were cool and relaxed. His dark eyes smouldered above his dark beard. He happened to be in one of his talkative moods tonight, talking non-stop while they drank orange squash on the cool stoep between dances.

He gave an account of all the local auctions. She only half listened. She suspected he was a spy, an informer, not to be trusted. Then again, she might be mistaken, he may indeed be nothing but a government official.

Has anything happened in the township recently? she asked casually.

"All hell broke out last weekend," he said, "until the captain stepped in and showed them a thing or two. He brought them under control all right." But what was her interest in the matter? he asked suspiciously.

(Under such firm control that he was bluish green in the face with the sheer effort of it, she thought.)

The music started up again. Round and round the dining room they went, the painted panels above their heads. The Kolyn fellow swept her round the floor with his usual vigorous strides, but Karolina was uninspired, nothing out of the ordinary would happen tonight. The dance was still pleasurable, she danced with infallible intuition, the man bristled with inexhaustible energy, but Karolina could not shake her sombre mood.

As they took another break outside on the stoep, under the small, sad lights, she thought that she would actually have preferred never to have been born at all.

The Kolyn fellow was unperturbed, he was not the sort of man to wonder about her mood changes.

After the dance she walked home slowly. It was a lovely night. Very clear. The moon was high. A plover called, the wind rose. As she was about to pass through the garden gate, she changed her mind. She walked over to Jess's house.

His appeared in the doorway, dark, inviting.

"How are you?" he asked gently.

"Oh," she said, "only so-so."

He looked down at her. Her mouth was dry. Her hair was stringy.

"Come," he said, and placed his warm hand on her neck.

"I don't feel well," she said, in a near whisper.

He drew her closer to him. She did not resist his embrace.

A breeze sprang up like rain, but it was a dry wind that only stirred the fallen leaves before dying down again.

"I've loved you from the very beginning," she heard him say close to her ear.

CHAPTER 14

"IT CAN BE unbearably painful to live within the moment," said Jess. "I've been trying to avoid it all my life, actually. But here, now, with you it is not hard to be present. This is where I want to be. I don't want to be anywhere else."

THE DAILY sweet late summer heralding of birds.

All at once there were large numbers of the butterfly species *Aloeides rileyi*.

The dark trickster *Aroa melanoleuca* appeared towards dusk, and the rare moth *Euproctis terminalis,* with its creamy white wings and thickly furred thorax and abdomen, was drawn to the light at night.

EVER SINCE she had received the letter from her sister, Karolina had not stopped thinking of her.

Karolina and her father had been interested in insects, but it seemed her sister considered invertebrates unworthy of her attention. She never showed an interest in anything equipped with a nervous system and blood circulation. Gentle, affectionate child that she was, she cared for nothing but stones.

This preference had finally taken her to one of the remotest corners of the earth. There, in an environment practically devoid of vegetation and inhabited by a mere handful of people, she studied rocks and meteorites.

Karolina had been her father's child, her sister had been their mother's. There had been a passionate bond between their mother and this child since early childhood—she had loved her with an intensity that their mother herself must have found alarming sometimes.

Their father had never bonded with his younger daughter in quite the same way as with Karolina. Perhaps her sister had been undesirable to him from the moment of her birth—perhaps he had wanted a son. Perhaps he could not come to terms with the child's unusual preoccupation, could not accept that he was unable to draw her into his world, so there had not been enough on which to build a relationship. Perhaps their incompatibility went deeper, was more difficult to formulate. Perhaps their mother had simply claimed this child for herself from the outset. Who knows?

Her sister had never spoken much. She had allowed their mother to hold on to her. She had submitted to being protected and adored. She had added more rocks to her collection, and one day she announced that she would be pursuing her research in a place very far from there.

Their mother had never recovered from the trauma caused by this loss. She had died two years before their father.

Karolina thought about her mother in a different way than about her father. Her grief about her mother was less acute, less intense, less time-bound. It was a grief that went back further, was more diffuse, and permeated her entire history.

CHAPTER 15

KAROLINA AND BASIL had dinner at the Springbok Café on Saturday night with Jess and Frans Roeg. She had danced with the Kolyn fellow in the hotel dining room the previous Saturday night, she had avoided the snooker room and the ladies' bar for the past two weeks, ever since Tonnie de Melck's death.

Frans was having a difficult time, Jess had said. She had asked if she could bring Basil along. (She was curious to know if he still put his money on the red one.)

The dining area at the Springbok Café was also screened off from the service area, but this section was much larger than its counterpart at the Rendezvous Café, with rows of high, wooden stools and low, red lights over the wooden table tops—an attempt at creating a cosy, intimate atmosphere.

Karolina had only just sat down when, looking over her shoulder, she saw Pol and company sitting across the room. (A merry little band of men—Karolina had never seen the slightest sign of a spouse at Pol's side, the heavy, gold wedding ring notwithstanding.) Pol gave her a suggestive wink charged with complicity. He shook his head lightly in mock surprise, as if unable to believe his good luck at the happy coincidence of their meeting there. He licked his lips pleasurably and raised his glass to his lips, but only after he had raised it almost imperceptibly to her.

Indeed Frans did seem to be having a difficult time. He drank excessively, and fast. He seemed to find it hard to focus on the conversation. At times he would simply sit there staring before him, as if at something that was being enacted before his mind's eye, his mouth twisted in an ironic smile.

Jess was more talkative than usual. He was tense, his colour was deep. He lowered his gaze as he spoke, his eyes shy behind his glasses, the eyelids heavy. (Karolina found it hard to reconcile this reserved, public gaze with the intimate openness of Jess's gaze when they made love.)

Basil and Karolina did not say much. Frans spoke of a film he had seen recently. Jess spoke of things she had never heard him speak of before, while they chewed their way through the thin steaks, the wilted lettuce leaves, and the enormous servings of potato chips.

The wry smile never left Frans's lips. Karolina remembered how he had sat all alone in the dark on the hotel stoep. (Was it he who had knocked at her hotel door that night?)

Basil avoided Karolina's gaze, he kept his eyes primly averted throughout. Karolina sat beside him, and Jess sat opposite her, next to Frans. She was impatient, she wanted to know what Basil was thinking.

On her way back from the toilet she ran into Pol in the narrow passage at the back. He took her hand in his, gazed deep into her eyes—the whites of his eyes no longer distinguishable from the irises.

"We belong together," he said feelingly, in a low voice.

She stared into his face. Fascinated by the mobility of it. The horizontality of its lines—the elongated eyes, nostrils and mouth. Every single feature caught up in a process of metamorphosis.

"We do," she said gently.

Still he held her hands in his. Tilted his head back slightly in order to observe her more closely. (With the swimming eyes.) His hair was wet with perspiration, his head was as sleek as an otter's. He looked at her long, wordlessly, eloquently.

"I felt it from the beginning," he said (swaying delicately to and fro; did he find it hard to remain upright?). "You and I were meant for each other."

"We were indeed," she said. Smiling. "Think of me while you make merry tonight," she said softly.

Once more he subjected her to a protracted look, his face glistening with perspiration. (She sometimes thought he had all the time in the world.)

"I am shuddering from head to toe at the thought of how I shall be thinking of you now," he said.

Before letting her hands go he squeezed them lightly, and went on his watery way.

(Soon he would start up the first song of the evening, and then depart with his jolly little band for more drinks at the ladies' bar.)

When Karolina returned to their table, Jess looked up briefly, staring straight into her eyes. The unexpected intimacy of his gaze made her blush deeply.

He spoke of flamingos, of unusual natural phenomena, of bartering systems in Central Africa, of computers. Now and then his eye would flicker anxiously over the whole company. Frans spoke of some other films he had seen recently. It seemed his imagination was stirred by themes tending to the macabre, to the sexually violent.

At times his observations were incisive, critical, focussed, then he would go off at a tangent once more. He was drinking steadily. In between drinks his forearm lay on the table entirely devoid of volition, glass in hand. Karolina noticed how vulnerable the inner arm seemed with its network of blue veins.

He was pale beneath the day-old stubble, his skin blotchy. His teeth were smallish for a man his size. When their eyes happened to meet, his gaze was sardonic, it was also reckless and sexual. She was startled and agitated by this. He did not seem to care whom he might be dragging down with him.

Basil was chewing on a matchstick. Though he remained silent, Karolina nevertheless had the impression that his attention was fixed unwaveringly on the conversation. He sat with his left elbow propped up on the table and his hand like a visor, shielding his eyes.

His lips were pressed together more firmly than usual, a tenseness at the corners of his mouth. She watched him from the corner of her eye.

After the meal they lingered briefly on the wide cement stoep before Basil walked Karolina home, and Jess and Frans walked off together.

The night air was cool, clean, a dove was cooing gently.

On her return to her room, Karolina sat down on the bed. She was agitated and restless. She leafed through her books.

She remained seated on the bed. The books were open beside her. She was suddenly overcome by a sense of longing, but also of loss. These two emotions seemingly almost indistinguishable .

Before putting out the light, she read the letter from her sister once more.

IN THE COURSE of the night she was woken by a gentle tap at her door (which opened out on the stoep). She assumed it was Jess. But when she peered through the window the dark figure outside was Frans Roeg.

As she opened the door, he had one hand pressed against the wall, and his jacket draped over the opposite shoulder.

He said nothing, merely looked at her with the wry half-smile. She remembered the night he had sat alone on the stoep, how she had wanted to go to him, yet at the same time had recoiled from him. She had a similar feeling now.

"What's wrong?" she asked softly.

Still he did not speak, he remained there standing upright, looking at her with the same impenetrable, cynical expression on his face. He had a bottle in one hand.

"I'm sorry," she said. "I can't see you now. I was already asleep when you knocked."

He shrugged, turned on his heel, and walked away.

She remained in the doorway listening to his footsteps on the gravel path—until she could no longer hear them.

She was upset. He had not said a word. She did not know what he had come for.

Jess woke her early the next morning with a tap at her door. She could tell something had happened even before he spoke.

"Frans was killed in an accident last night," he said.

"DID YOU KNOW it would happen?" she asked Basil.

"Yes," he said.

They had been sitting under the willow tree all morning.

"I suppose there was nothing you could have said to warn him in any way?" she said.

"No," said Basil. "It was upon him already. There was no way he could escape it."

THAT AFTERNOON Karolina lay on her bed. She wondered what the signs might have been. She never really got to know Frans, she thought. There had been some attraction, she had thought of him in erotic terms, had weighed him up as a potential lover. It had not led to anything more, and better that way. What had appeared in the sky for him? At dusk? At the rising of the new moon? When the sky is clear and there is no wind, if a sudden gust should spring from nowhere, then you know, Basil told her. When the sky takes on a triangular or a spherical form, then death follows inevitably. Did she really need to know these things? About the colour and shape of the sky? Oh, Lord. The short-term signs—black tannin accumulating at the base of the teeth, the bridge of the nose caving in, a persistent urge to stretch the limbs, the eyes staring unblinkingly, the cheeks caving in, tears flowing unrestrainedly, the lobes of the ears collapsing towards the head, the urine emitting wispy fumes. If Frans had recognised the signs himself, what would he have done? He obviously no longer cared a damn. Had been drinking himself into a stupor. Had he been sexually irresponsible as well? Who had been his most recent companion anyway? The beautiful woman, the most beautiful woman Jess had ever seen? Would Frans have avoided all meaningless activity, had he known? Would he have purified his spirit in anticipation? Not very likely. He looked like someone who had ceased to believe in a positive outcome. He seemed dangerous, as if he had ceased to care about anyone else. Had wanted to drag others down with him. There was something compelling about it. Had he remained committed to anything? To the woman he loved? To his own pain? He could no longer have been attached to life very firmly. He was not even speaking any more. Words had become superfluous, too difficult, or too unreliable. He had lost faith in words—words no longer had the power to bind him to life. He had shrugged his shoulders and walked away until the sound of his footsteps had faded away.

ON SUNDAY NIGHT a restless wind blew. It sent the leaves scuttling along the streets. Clouds moved rapidly past the moon.

Jess came to visit, he spoke of Frans.

"I think nobody really knew him," he said. "He wasn't on intimate terms with anyone. It's a story of decline. At one point everything seemed so promising. They were living in a beautiful place just outside the city. Then they moved away because she felt it was too isolated."

Jess was sprawled on the bed on his side, he spoke musingly. "There was one thing after another. His situation at work was difficult; problems arose within the relationship. He began to drink more. At every turn the noose was tightening. He became more closed off."

Jess stared in front of him. "And there was more to it than that. Things he brought into the relationship—into every single one of his relationships. We all do—but there was such a deep-rooted contradiction within him, such discord. Such an obvious dark side to him. He was so extraordinarily inconstant. We were fairly close, yet I felt I had no idea of his basic drives. More so than with most people, his deepest fantasies remained hidden—he never gave the slightest hint of what they might be. Nothing but this persistent fascination with violence—this obsession with every manifestation of sex and violence."

Jess exhaled slowly through the mouth, and drew another deep breath. "Whenever I think of Frans, all sorts of primitive images come to mind," he said.

Let's leave now, let's leave this place behind tonight, Karolina wanted to say. I want to go away with you. Perhaps we were meant for each other. Tomorrow it may be your turn, or mine. Tonight it is close enough—this reminder of mortality. But it may come closer still, much closer.

Jess sighed. He covered his face with his hand. He lay in this position for a while, on his side, his weight on his elbow, his right hand covering his face.

"One can think of a dead person in one of two ways," he said. "Firstly, that he has simply ceased to exist. Secondly, that a living person has been transformed into a non-living person. Strange to think that he should still be lying there somewhere. Or not really him. But him, nevertheless."

This, too, was her very thought—that Frans, or what used to be Frans—was lying in the small Avbob building.

Karolina got up to draw the curtain. Jess's mood was affecting her. She had never known him to be this subdued and depressed before. He would have to leave. Pursue his turbid meditations elsewhere. She felt resentful, she disliked seeing him so uncentred, so troubled.

A large stick insect (order *Phasmida*, from phasma, an apparition) perched on a fold in the curtain. She blew on it lightly, but it refused to fly away. She blew more fiercely, shaking the curtain lightly, but the insect refused to go out into the night, her stick-like legs retaining their grip.

Tonight Karolina would have preferred Jess and herself to smile upon each other in complete accord, to regard each other trustingly, to embrace with burning passion. Why should they be unable this night to reach out to each other, surrendering fully to physical love, without the intrusive, improper thought of death coming between them?

BOTH OF THEM were caught unawares by Jess's mood of despondency. "I didn't realise I could still be overwhelmed to this extent," he said.

Karolina made no reply.

"It's not as bad as it used to be," he said. "Before, I would have been affected much more than this. But still, I am depressed. Frans's death probably triggered it. A keener sense of mortality. Of loss and of mourning. Of unfulfilled dreams. Of all one's cherished dreams coming to nothing. Of labouring under illusions all one's life. What did Frans's life amount to—what has become of his dreams?"

They were sitting in the Rendezvous Café. Karolina had her elbow on the table, her chin propped in her hand. Her head was turned away from Jess slightly. She did not speak.

"Frans's death has stirred up old emotions," he said, "mourning and loss are some of my most deep-seated feelings. Behind these feelings I have a sense of other, earlier experiences of loss. Every loss implies an earlier loss."

"Where does it all start?" asked Karolina, without looking at him.

"Oh, I suppose it goes back a long way," Jess replied.

He was leaning back slightly in his chair. His long legs (sturdy calves) were stretched out before him.

She kept her gaze averted from him. She knew his sprawled body would appeal to her irresistibly even now—she had but to look at him.

In love Karolina's senses became acute and her memory was all but obliterated. Love made her impatient. In the veld every morning she was silent, and in the afternoons she slept heavily.

She had stopped putting her faith in Beyers and Delarey. She knew they were organising in the township, but whatever they might be doing was their affair.

At night the soles of her feet grew unbearably hot.

ON FRIDAY NIGHT, three weeks after Tonnie de Melck had lost his head in the ladies' bar, Karolina ventured into the snooker room again. She went there by herself.

She kept an unobtrusive watch on those present, trying to determine the possible effects on them of De Melck's death. Nothing to be seen on the surface. Everyone was carrying on as usual, pissing and prattling away; each with his own impulses, resolutions, little schemes.

Kieliemann was his usual, persistent self. As the evening progressed (the dramatis personae waiting in the wings), as the rhythm of disintegration and convergence gathered momentum, he would press the swelling bulge against her buttocks with ever greater urgency, pawing and groping wherever he could lay his hands on her.

He ambushed her in the corridor leading to the toilets, pressed himself against her, and pleaded in her neck.

"Come with me tonight," he said. "Drop the little hotnot. Why do you lie about with him all day? Don't think everybody doesn't know."

Karolina pushed him away fiercely, rapidly crossed the snooker room, the ladies' bar, the lounge, then the baroque reception area, leaving through the front door. The night was cool.

Behind her, on the dark stoep, she imagined Frans Roeg sitting at a table alone. He did not speak, he merely smiled and raised his glass to her in a sensual, seductive gesture.

She did not look round, she walked home as fast as she could.

ON SUNDAY MORNING she was sitting on the stoep alone with a drink, when the red car pulled up outside the hotel. Adelia and Fernes were there, they had come back, they had come for the picnic.

CHAPTER 16

ADELIA AND FERNES had returned from their travels. They were full of stories and anecdotes. What a country, they said, what a terrifying, overwhelming country. The things that were happening here! Terrible, horrendous things. They were still unable to make proper sense of it. It was so unlike the bizarre nightmarishness of certain large American cities.

On Sunday morning they went for a picnic at the spruit with Basil and Karolina.

They spread their rugs under the willow tree, and took out the food.

"Oh," cried Adelia, reclining on some cushions, "we are in a meadow! The meadow has been part of the geography of bliss since medieval times!"

As he feared the desolation of the veld, Fernes did not feel at ease immediately. They had brought a tape recorder, and Adelia suggested he should put on some music, it would help him to relax. Fernes did so, playing a recording of Bach flute sonatas.

They unpacked the delectables on a white table cloth. The silver, the cut glass, the crockery, the starched linen napkins.

"Heirlooms," said Adelia. "Gifts from the family."

She took out the cheeses, the loaves, the cold meats, the caviar, the fruit, the wine, the champagne. She cut the melons, she slit the watermelon that groaned and split open crisply in a lush display of opulent black seeds set in intimate pink flesh—resembling the fruit in her paintings.

"I believe in the surface, I believe one hundred per cent in the surface," she said. "I believe in nothing but the surface. Show me what lies behind it!"

(Fernes made a playful pretence of exposing himself.)

Adelia wore her pearls and a white embroidered silk frock. Her rich, heavy hair was tied back, leaving her pale, intense face quite exposed. She was still on the mend from her back injury, she told them.

Fernes wore the most exotic shirt and sandals Karolina had ever seen on any man's body and feet, his hair was raven black, a profusion of curls sprouted from his temples, and a love lock lay sensuously in the nape of his neck. His gaze shifted restlessly across the open landscape.

Once more they expressed regret at not being able to speak Afrikaans, and Karolina said she regretted not being able to speak Spanish.

Adelia poured the wine into crystal glasses. The wine reminded her, she said, of something she had read recently. Some seventeenth century South American female mystics believed they were able to receive divine love and mystical knowledge directly, through the mouth—or through the mouth of the soul, words being superfluous. María de San Joseph described how the mouth of her soul had penetrated the wound of Jesus, and how she had drunk copiously of his warm blood—it seemed María de San Joseph was frequently invited to drink the Lord.

(Fernes bared his canines like Nosferatu, gesturing obscenely as he did so.)

"Drinking the blood of Christ in this way," Adelia said, "represents a significant reversal of menstruation—the essential female weakness."

Basil was lying on his back, chewing on a blade of grass. His wine was balanced on his chest.

"This act of attaching oneself to the Sacred Body represents something more than mere eroticism," she said, "it is also a denial of phallocentrism. There is a deliberate focus on those parts of the body that are not primarily associated with male sexuality."

"More wine?" Fernes asked Karolina.

"The language of mysticism is the language of desire, but without the implication of sublimated sexuality."

She broke the bread, and passed a piece to each of them. "This is the best on offer at the local café," she said. "Not particularly impressive." She put cheese on her bread and ate hungrily.

Fernes was a good actor. Mimicking people and recounting certain situations seemed temporarily to harness his great restlessness—constantly threatening to blow up everything in the immediate vicinity.

Adelia said Fernes would sing to them in a little while. The Bach sonatas came to an end, and he put on more music. Karolina asked about it. It was Monteverdi, said Fernes. They ate and they drank. Adelia and Fernes spoke, Basil and Karolina listened. It was hot, time was passing slowly.

One of her fantasies, said Adelia, piling oysters on a piece of bread, one of her greatest fantasies was to be served by others. She had no desire for material things, she wanted to be served. To be picked up and dropped off by chauffeurs. To have people do things for her. She had no desire for material possessions, she would be perfectly happy to stay in hotels for the rest of her days—she liked hotel rooms, they were so impersonal. She did not need to be surrounded by personal possessions. A few mementoes would do. Photographs of her lovers. Some reproductions.

As the day progressed, it grew steadily hotter. They drew more deeply into the shade. The ants (order *Hymenoptera*, family *Formicidae*) came after their food. The cicadas (order *Hemiptera*, family *Cicadidae*) shrilled deafeningly. The veld was dry but fragrant, filled with the high-pitched sounds of innumerable insects. Beyond these sounds the silence was almost tangible.

They were sitting peacefully in the veld, in the middle of a vast plain to the northeast of the Brandwater Basin—in the heart of what used to be an arena of endless conflict. The sky was remote and insubstantial, the horizon vibrated, melting into the veld. There were small clouds at eye level. The sky was constantly changing, if one cared to observe it.

Karolina noticed Adelia's hands—they were strong and not very large, but the fingernails were small, they resembled her sister's nails. This brought unexpected tears to her eyes.

Adelia and Fernes spoke of their journey, of relations they had visited in the Transvaal (Adelia's uncle on her father's side). They recounted anecdotes and incidents from their past, they told of their first meeting, they spoke of countries they had visited, of Bogotá, where they lived, of places they meant to visit. They spoke of books, of music, of painters. Adelia spoke about her work. She spoke of her childhood—of visits to South Africa, of visits to this region.

Fernes played motets by Orlando di Lasso and Cristóbal de Morales, five-part madrigals by Gesualdo.

They interrupted each other and enlarged on each other's stories. In conversation they were like a pair of trapeze artists, releasing and catching hold of each other in midair with impeccable timing.

A beetle (order *Coleoptera*—the largest order in the whole of the animal kingdom, family *Scarabaeidae*) rolled her ball of dung in the hot, languorous hour of the scarab. Stark-eyed locusts (order *Orthoptera*, family *Acrididae*) clung to swaying stalks of grass. Huge brown and black centipedes (class *Diplopoda*, distinct from the class *Insecta*, though both belonged to the phylum *Arthropoda*) moved by slowly in the hot sand like diminutive trains.

The banks of the spruit were dry, but Karolina knew about their stores of clay when it rained.

Adelia picked up a centipede. She looked at it long and attentively.

"At school the boys used to put silkworms on their tongues," said Karolina.

"Oh, men!" said Adelia. "Men are obsessed with the phallus from the moment they're born. They want to stick it in everywhere all the time. There is nothing in this world they don't see in terms of the phallus."

Basil lay on his side, he was laughing soundlessly.

Fernes made as if to put the centipede in his mouth.

Karolina remembered building clay kraals for the centipedes with a little boy she used to play with (using the clay in the banks of the spruit).

They ate the cheese, they ate the bread, they ate the caviar, the oysters, the firm tomatoes, the tangy radishes, the green cucumber. Adelia used a knife and fork to eat the glowing pink watermelon. Karolina wondered if this was how it was done in Colombia.

Adelia said of course men were granted a greater degree of freedom than women. Unlike men, women were expected to stay well within the limits imposed by society. For men there were no limits! Women faced a far greater threat of being excluded from society, of becoming pariahs. Female sexuality was far more likely to be stigmatised. For this reason women were compelled to move within a more narrowly circumscribed space.

She sank back into the cushions. Her hot face bore traces of pain. A woman had to be more cautious about the signs transmitted by her body, she said, once certain limits were overstepped, she'd had it. Unlike men, a woman could not abuse whisky, sperm, sex.

"In addition," she said, "men have always had the freedom and the authority to hold office, to occupy public space. During the seventeenth century the mystical experience opened up a potential space for women, giving them a similar freedom of movement, albeit imaginary. A space within which their transgressive desire might take shape."

Basil asked if her back was hurting.

Yes, said Adelia, she was in constant pain.

Would she object to taking something to ease the pain? he asked.

Not in the least, she said, she had great faith in medication, all medication, painkillers, antidepressants, anything at all. She believed in all forms of therapy, physical or psychical. She had no fear of medicine or treatment of any kind. "And it's just as well," she added.

Basil rummaged in the pouch and came up with a small phial. She thrust back her head and he placed some tiny tablets on her tongue.

Fernes was approaching a state of advanced mental disquiet—he was like a great bird of prey coming in to land after a long flight, unable to find a tree.

"Mystic language," said Adelia, "engages metaphors of fire and water, of burning, of melting, of thirst, and of drinking."

Fernes poured himself a huge glass of chilled strawberry juice.

It was the hottest time of day. Everything was finely and precisely poised in a delicate balance—the heat vibrations at the far horizon, the short, jagged shadows, the unvarying sounds of insects.

Fernes played the Stabat Mater by Pergolesi. The searingly sweet, tortured, and yet erotic female voices spiralled up into the sky, beyond these indescribable sounds lay the silence of the open veld.

"Aestheticised pain," said Adelia.

Dark clouds were gathering at the horizon to the left of them and Karolina imagined she had caught a glimpse of a movement to their right—a head appearing briefly above the bank of the spruit.

"I suspect we're being watched," she told Basil. "It must be Kieliemann and company."

"Must be," said Basil, unperturbed, not moving.

She briefed Adelia and Fernes on the situation. Adelia stood up and walked slowly to the bank of the spruit. She stood there defiantly for some time, scanning the surrounding veld.

"Come on out!" she cried. "Come out! Arrest us! Torture the truth out of us!"

The echo of her cry resounded in the distance. Then all was silent once more. There was a noise some distance away, a loose scuttling, a sound of rolling clods, and a rustle of dry grass.

"Bullies," she said as she sat down once again. "Cowards. Misogynists. Police. They're the same everywhere."

Basil was still lying on his back. Fernes was dozing. Adelia was watching the horizon.

"I'm an atheist," she said, "but I have great respect for the mystics. I'm drawn to them. If I were a believer and a Catholic, I would have no difficulty accepting the Pope as my spiritual father. And if my life depended on it, I would convert to any religion under the sun."

It had grown extremely hot. Karolina, too, was lying on her back. Watching the clouds. Listening to Adelia's warm, ironic voice; she had started singing softly in a foreign tongue. Fernes was fast asleep. Basil had turned over on his stomach.

"Nothing shocks me, and everything shocks me, do you understand that?" Adelia asked Karolina. "Emotionally I am in a state of perpetual rawness, of chronic devastation. I am continually appalled and nauseated by the ways of the world."

She picked up a dry land shell, she pressed it softly to her cheek, then placed it carefully next to a tomato.

"At the same time I have a constant urge to tell the world— against my better judgement: 'Come on! Shock me! Show me how everything is connected, and how perverted it is!'"

The mass of clouds to their left was growing darker. Basil sat up.

"Do you smell the rain?" asked Karolina.

Fernes was roused from his deep slumber. He also sat up and looked round, glancing at his watch.

"Six kilometres away," Basil said.

Adelia asked Fernes to sing, and he sang a Colombian Indian song expressing the natives' distrust of the white settlers along the coast. He had a sonorous voice and he sang beautifully.

Clouds were gathering, but it was still very hot.

"Let's dance," said Adelia when the song had ended.

There, in the dry bed of the spruit, in the middle of the small, sandy depression, the four of them danced to the stately rhythm of Renaissance music. They danced slowly and with great deliberation. Adelia, keeping an upright posture, danced with great restraint. Soon they were dripping with perspiration. Their feet were covered in dust. The clay stored in the banks of the spruit was waiting to be liberated, to become clay.

Karolina felt a flow of energy rising steadily in her calves. She felt her legs grow strong, her spine grow supple. She was sucking up strength from the hot, dusty earth, she was drawing it into the marrow of her bones.

They danced until the first raindrops came down, until the rain came down in force. They bundled the picnic things together hurriedly, and ran to the car in the pouring rain.

They drove along the steamy, wet streets and into the town, past the cemetery, where the rain beat down on stone monuments, on the tiny graves of children, and on the fresh grave of the younger De Melck—piled high with flowers—hidden from the gaze of passers-by.

They pulled up outside the hotel. In the lounge they had a drink to warm themselves and later they had dinner under the painted panels in the dining room. Adelia could not take her eyes off them.

"Somewhere I, too, have a part in this history," she said. "I shall come back soon. I shall return here to record this landscape. Down to the last detail."

THE NEXT MORNING Adelia and Fernes departed.

They were due to return within a week to Bogotá, Colombia, on the Meta River that arises in the highlands of Venezuela.

Karolina had a lump in the back of her throat, it ached.

When they said goodbye, Adelia held her close. "Don't be sad," she said gently, close to Karolina's ear, "it's never easy, but we're friends, I shall never let you down. Beyond this parting lies our happy reunion."

Karolina held Adelia's hands in hers—she studied the tiny, fan-shaped nails. As she embraced her once more, she shut her eyes, and found in Adelia's hair the scent of her beloved sister.

When they pulled away, there was no dust, since the streets were wet with rain.

CHAPTER 17

IT RAINED all week. It was an unseasonal, belated, useless rain—the crops were ruined by now—but it was gratifying nevertheless. It brought some relief, it was a diversion, an event. It put an end to the strain of many months. It was a sign, a pledge, a token of grace. God's bountiful rain—invoked by the young minister at the funeral of Tonnie de Melck—that the souls had thirsted for like sun-scorched clods.

All of a sudden there were more people in town. The whites emerged from their holes like termites. The local farmers drove their pickup trucks into town every morning, stopped in at the Rendez-vous Café for coffee. They bought wilted fruit and magazines before leaving. Cosmetics sales at the two chemist's shops were better than they had been for a long time. The black inhabitants fell back silently before the joyous white invasion. The doors of Nelson's Funeral Par-lour were thrown open invitingly.

Karolina and Basil did not go out into the veld on Monday. They sat drinking tea at the Rendezvous Café all morning, they walked about in town. They had coffee in the hotel lounge towards the end of the morning. They had lunch, and even the six heroic landscapes seemed different today—milder, mellower, more lyrical.

Hippopotami frolicked among the reeds in the foreground of one of the two panels depicting the idyllic life; the landscape in the background was one of great and unspoilt beauty. A Zulu kraal set in a vast, mountainous landscape was depicted in the other panel—a primordial landscape of peace and plenty, with plump, green calabashes scattered among the huts in the foreground, and rounded, undulating hills fading into the distance among the mighty cliffs that rose on either side.

Karolina was filled with anticipation at the prospect of seeing Jess again.

Towards dusk, when the rain let up somewhat, and the wet streets were steaming with heat, the flying ants emerged. One by one the fliers, male and female, spread their wings and took flight. They had picked up the signal. They ascended in dense clouds from deep within the earth. Thousands upon thousands of brides and grooms took off on their nuptial flight. The sky was filled with a soft whirring of wings and with signals imperceptible to the human ear. After mating, the female starts a new nest. The first eggs are nourished by the fat reserves stored in her own body and by the remains of her flight muscles, which she will never use again since from now on she is to do nothing but produce eggs for the remainder of her life.

NIGHTS OF SEARING intimacy now followed for Karolina and Jess.

They admitted no barriers between them, they reached out to each other in impatient surrender.

Karolina welcomed the bitter intensity of transient erotic pleasure. She pursued it! She embraced it! She reached out for the fleeting bliss of every night.

She had allowed herself to be led astray by extravagant predictions, and she submitted to the inevitable outcome.

WHEN THE HEAVIEST rain was over, Karolina and Basil went out into the crisp, sweet-smelling veld again.

"Do you remember the man we picked up after the accident?" she asked him. "The blood that spurted from his leg was so incredibly bright. I'd never seen anything quite like it."

"I remember," said Basil.

"I wonder what really happened there that day," said Karolina. She passed a brown paper bag to Basil. "That was the day we saw Beyers and Delarey in the café," she said.

"Yes," said Basil.

"And the poor dead guy in the pickup truck," she said. "The lawyer."

She was squatting on her haunches next to Basil. (This was how she used to squat next to her father in the veld.) He was scraping dirt off a smallish land shell. There was a different feel to the veld today. The light seemed changed after the rain.

"Are all these events connected somehow?" she asked.

"Yes," replied Basil, "they are."

CHAPTER 18

AFTER THE RAIN the veld was full of surprises again, and so was the snooker room (one never knew what to expect there).

The timid veld flowers gave up their hidden medicinal properties, and whenever Karolina raised her head, the sky would open up wide like a china-blue fan.

The snooker room continued to be a place where one could lose one's bearings, a cosy place. The snooker table was a bed of luscious green. A green surface in which to go astray; green as grass or green as venom, lichen green or leaf green, shit green or tender green, depending on the hour, the light, on the density of the smoke, on the talk and the behaviour of those present, on the phase of the moon, or on the nature of one's hopes and fears. Karolina could never keep away from it for long.

She ignored Kieliemann, she sat calmly next to Basil on the cane seat in the corner, she drank whisky, and she played when it was her turn.

Her shoulders were soft and delicately rounded under the light, covered in a layer of sweat as fine as the dust on the wings of moths; her hair glowed, it was on fire, it formed a dark aureole about her head. She was like a woman with a secret. Her secret set her apart, it surrounded her like a delicate vapour. Her skin was warm and moist.

Basil sat by her side, imperturbable as always, his lips closed in an expression of mock seriousness or pressed together quite firmly, depending on the circumstance. He exuded a sense of inner well-being.

Next door, in the ladies' bar, Pol's sonorous voice sounded up in song upon song, and the magistrate with his webbed hands sat in the opposite corner, sipping his drink.

KAROLINA HAD a dream of an orange-coloured locust. The insect was soft, the articulations of its body were of felt, not of hard, chitinous ectoplasm. The body was flexible, fused, not divided into thorax and abdomen, and the legs were not articulated. The locust perched on a dark, orange-coloured flower next to her bed, which was in a pale room. It moved across the flower with a silky sound (with a rustle of silk). It did not eat the flower but passed rapidly over it, destroying it, alighting on something else. The blighted flower remained in the glass, its petals turned brown. The locust looked at her with round, soft, orange-coloured eyes—a look of understanding in its eyes.

JESS HAD A DREAM of a bird with the most remarkable, brilliant, cellophane-like feathers. In his hands the entire magnificent plumage suddenly came off, so the bird was completely naked. He then put the little parcel of bright feathers back on again.

The meaning of the dream was probably tied up with narcissistic repair, with a redress of castration, he said. First there is an injury to the self as phallus, then the dream makes good this damage done to the self.

"THERE ARE THOSE whose symptoms result from some sort of trauma, or shock, or sorrow, or from early emotional abuse, or deprivation of a kind," said Basil.

"Someone like this is cold. His head is cold—as if it is packed in ice. His sweat is cold, there are drops of cold sweat on his forehead. His skin is cold to the touch, even his breath is cold. His face is pale, it may be bluish even, the eyes are sunken, the features frozen. He sweats profusely. All his excretions are excessive—vomiting, diarrhoea, urine, saliva, sweat. He has a sensation sometimes of something live stirring in his gut, he feels as if his innards are all knotted up, as if cold water runs in his veins—the pain and discomfort of this can drive him crazy.

"He is restless; he feels quite desperate at times, he broods all by himself. He is tired of life, he is critical and depressed, he despairs of his place in the world, he is constantly anticipating misfortune. He can get very angry if interfered with. He is treacherous, he lies—he tells outrageous lies. He has a great need to destroy things, to cut them up, to rip them to pieces, sometimes to the point of wiping them out completely. In the worst of these cases he eats his own faeces—his own shit. This urge can be as powerful as the need to destroy—which is exceptionally strong in these people.

"That's the kind of man," Basil said, "Gert Els is."

CHAPTER 19

ON THE DAY Adelia and Fernes arrived in Bogotá, Colombia, Karolina and Basil saw the lovers in the cemetery again.

It was the end of March, and no longer as hot during the midday hour. There were intimations of autumn in the air. They passed the cemetery on their way back from the veld and Karolina told Basil she would like to see Tonnie de Melck's grave. Basil asked if she knew where it was. She said no, she didn't, but she would look for it. It was sure to have already been marked in some way.

They were going down the path, past the two tall cypresses, in the direction of the new extension, when they saw two people some distance away.

They were the lovers, and they were standing by a grave. His arm was around her waist.

"It's Jurie Beyers and the woman," Karolina said. "I'm convinced they're standing at De Melck's grave."

Karolina and Basil walked back some of the way and at Karolina's suggestion sat down on a bench close to one of the giant cypresses. "I want to see them," she said. They sat in silence. After a while the lovers began to walk slowly up the path. Their pace was measured, meditative. Jurie Beyers was speaking quietly to the woman, she was listening attentively. His arm was still around her waist.

It was a slow, exclusive, intimate walk, they were receptive to nothing but each other and the moment. Beyers spoke quietly, urgently, his head close to hers; she kept her gaze on the ground before her feet.

They came to a sudden stop in the middle of the path. It was very quiet all around. The light was changing, it was less harsh. The woman raised her face to look at him, he cradled it in his hands and gazed at her for a long time.

Karolina and Basil remained sitting on the bench. She gazed up at the sky. It was absolutely, heart-rendingly clear.

The lovers remained like this for a while, then resumed their walk. When they came close to Karolina and Basil, both of them looked in their direction, aware of their presence for the first time.

For a few moments Beyers stared at Basil fixedly—then he nodded briefly in their direction and walked past. (His expression less guarded than the last time Karolina had seen him in the ladies' bar.) The woman stared at them briefly, apprehensively. She did not greet them.

Once more there was an expression of great sadness on her face, it was as poignantly beautiful as it had been the first time Karolina had seen them, which had been right here, in the cemetery.

Karolina knew as little now as she had known before of the exact circumstances that caused the lovers to be banished to this remote corner of town, but their relationship now seemed to be taking on a grim significance, a fatal intensity that had been lacking before.

KAROLINA AND JESS talked about Frans Roeg. Karolina was lying in Jess's arm, the moon visible from where they were lying. The night air was becoming much chillier. She was grateful for the warmth of his body.

"Was his death an accident?" she asked.

"It's hard to tell," replied Jess. "It seems there was nothing really to make his life worth living. He was in love with this woman, and the relationship was foundering. She was unpredictable, she was very depressed at times. Very beautiful, very depressed. A complicated person. That didn't make things easier for him. I don't know that they were seeing much of each other lately. She had bouts of wanting to cut herself off from the world completely. In a fit of religious mania, almost. He found it very trying, given his outspoken lack of faith. He was drinking heavily. He was depressed about the political situation."

Karolina's face was turned towards the window. Jess, she knew, was looking at the wall as he spoke. Against this wall was the Tibetan tanka depicting Yama, the lord of death, against the black backdrop of non-existence.

"Given these circumstances, I don't know if his death was altogether an accident," he said.

She turned her gaze on his warm, dark profile.

"He grew reckless. He drank too much, he drove too fast, he probably didn't give a damn any more."

Karolina lay there pondering Frans's death. It was the exact moment of transition from life to death that she could not grasp.

AUTUMN ANNOUNCED itself radiantly in the streets of the town. (Sharper at the edges in the early morning and towards evening.)

Karolina and Basil played snooker, and on Saturday night she danced the tango with the Kolyn fellow in the hotel dining room below the six painted panels.

The tango, that perverse, tragic, triumphant dance that originated among the alienated and uprooted inhabitants of the slums of Buenos Aires.

She was waiting for a letter from Adelia, in confirmation of their friendship.

BEFORE GOING to the snooker room on Friday evening, Karolina went to the ladies' bar for a drink. She wanted to talk to Pol. He was already sitting in the usual corner with his companions. The bar was quite empty and she had only just ordered her drink when he made a silent appearance by her left elbow.

"Beloved," he said.

She turned towards him. He studied her silently.

"What's up?" she asked.

"The lads are turning nasty," he said.

"What is the theatrical company doing?" she asked.

Pol gave her an appraising look.

"Those lads have a tendency to spread themselves thinly," said Pol. (Karolina thought of Jurie Beyers and the woman in tender conversation in the cemetery.)

"And Gert Els?" she asked.

"Our very own captain," said Pol, "is but one of many." He took a swig from his glass. "An exceptionally disagreeable specimen nevertheless. That lad is known to strike quickly, and he doesn't allow anyone to fool around with him. The temper is short and the impulses violent."

Pol smiled amiably.

"Personally, I have no great urge to get mixed up in his affairs," he said.

"But it's been like that ever since I first arrived here," she said.

He fixed her with his watery gaze.

"But in the meanwhile a few lads have bitten the dust," he said.

They drank in silence.

"Tell me now," said Pol, "of all you have come across since you arrived here."

"Oh," said Karolina. "Many things. I've learnt a great deal since coming here."

"I shudder all over at the thought of everything you have come to know about," said Pol.

He gave her a penetrating look, intimate, the elongated eyes brimming. He put his head right up against hers. She felt the damp of his intense body heat. "Here, right here, where our great general once led the battle?" he asked in low, conspiratorial tones.

"Yes," she said.

He rocked to and fro on his feet.

"Are we yet again to discern the hand of God in all of this?" he asked. He studied her at length, head tilted to one side, his gaze contemplative.

She smiled. "It's possible," she said.

He shook his head gently, as if wanting to rid himself of a nasty suspicion. The magistrate in his corner emitted a high-pitched neigh. (Karolina glanced in his direction with distaste).

"By the way," she said (her eyes wandering to the zebra skin on the rear wall), "how is the widow doing?"

"She comes from an old family," Pol said. "Her grandfather happened to be one of the lads who roamed the area just this side of the Brandwater Basin with De Wet."

Pol peered deep into the past before turning his gaze on Karolina again.

"I shudder to think of how those lads roamed all over the place," he said. "Hardly more than a hundred miles from here."

"But the woman," she said, "what were you saying about her?"

Pol shook his head slowly from side to side.

"That poor lad did not know the end of his sorrows," he said. And this was as much as he was prepared to say.

"Do you ever work?" she asked suddenly.

He gave her a grave look, wiped his face with a handkerchief. "The interests of this town—which happen always to be threatened—are under constant protection, thanks to the legal astuteness of Pol Habermaut & Partners," he said.

She finished her whisky, took leave of Pol, and went off to play a game of snooker in the cosy room next door with its treacherous green surface, its sulphurous emissions, its antelope trophies, beer posters, and framed photographs of the two Free State snooker champions: Horace van Deventer and Stick Conradie.

Lieutenant Kieliemann looked up when she entered, salivating at the sight of her, but otherwise remaining as expressionless as ever.

ON SATURDAY NIGHT she danced with the Kolyn fellow. Out on the stoep between dances the string of multicoloured lights was stirred by a small, chilly breeze. The positions of the stars had changed, it was no longer the night sky of summer.

Tonight they did the tango with a languor, a lingering suggestion of passion, surpassing the highest expectations of those present.

The Kolyn fellow never missed a beat, he did his utmost—met Karolina with all the skill and technical expertise at his disposal. His long, slim feet were neatly shod in the lace-up ankle sneakers, he was wearing short trousers, his hairy (but elegant) calves were flexed to the extreme, his shoulder blades wet with perspiration, his dark Voortrekker beard neatly trimmed. He danced impeccably but mechanically, with just the faintest touch of an erotic edge to his movements. His interpretation of the tango was military, he did it with abrupt precision, switchblade footwork. Karolina danced with restrained carnality, her movements steeped in nostalgia and love.

Tonight the dance was a heavily stylised form of sexual encounter—legs sliding suggestively in between legs, Karolina's body snapping in sensual provocation. Although they were both dancing with restrained energy, their movements had a flavour of recklessness, a disquieting hint of foreboding, that sent nervous shivers through the other dancers.

After the dance Karolina walked home slowly. The night air lay cool on her warm skin.

On the way she observed three moth species of the family *Sphingidae*: the sweet potato bee moth (*Agrius convolvuli*), the death's head moth (*Acherontia atropos*), and the oleander bee moth (*Deilephila*).

She paused a while to look at the large, well-camouflaged oleander bee moth—to the unsuspecting eye it was almost invisible. It was one of her favourite moths. The extremities of the wings and the tapering tip of the conspicuous abdomen formed a triangle. The wings resembled marbled paper, the colour was deep, the texture sensual—velvet browns and fern greens tinged pink.

How extraordinary, she thought, to encounter these three species in the course of a single night. Should she consider herself lucky, or should it be taken as a warning?

SHE SPENT THE whole of Sunday lying on her bed. The previous night she had recklessly surrendered to the dance, today she was thinking about her life in the city. There, too, she had lain on her bed in much the same way, staring out of the window. In much the same way, yet differently. There she had felt herself cut off from the world and her mood was often sombre. Outside, the enormous banana and pawpaw leaves were unfurling. At times the sky was leaden, at other times it was clear; it was always hot. Humid. Claustrophobic. She had felt hemmed in, restricted. These restraints were self-imposed. Or due to the pressure of circumstance. She had stared at the leaves from below—they were huge, their green surfaces glowed with an exceptional intensity. Around her everything was green, luxuriant, exotic. Everything grew rapidly, and decomposed equally rapidly—all life cycles were accelerated: germination, maturation and fruition, and death. Her own rhythm was slower. She had lain on her bed motionless, staring at the growing, unfolding leaves.

Had anything changed since then? She had been closed off. She had kept herself closed off for a long time from the tenderness of embrace. She had removed herself to a different plane.

She came here. Her dedication to the moths brought her here. She gave Basil a lift on the way. She had her palm read by the spectacular light of the setting sun. The woman put some farfetched ideas into her head.

She surrendered to Jess's embrace. She surrendered to her own desire.

Love made her reckless. It made her impatient. It turned her into a woman she did not recognise. At times it made her desperate and anxious. At times she wanted to crawl back to the shelter of the huge leaves below the oppressive, leaden sky of the city.

Why do you sometimes cut yourself off from me? Jess asked.

She could not answer him. The meandering route she had come along was impossible to retrace.

JESS ASKED HER to go away with him for a few days. He needed a break, he said; he was getting nowhere with his research. This time she accepted his invitation without hesitation.

They drove to the little dorp Klaarte, ninety kilometres south of Voorspoed. They did not rush, but stopped frequently, had tea along the way. Karolina was glad to be with Jess, she was happy.

Towards dusk they arrived at Klaarte, on the Klaar River. They checked into a hotel. They had a meal in the dining room and retired to their room early. It had been too dark on their arrival to see much of the town, they would have to wait until the following morning.

Being in the room suddenly made Karolina anxious. She had a sudden sense of panic. It was urgent that she should know what it looked like outside, what the town was like.

She stood at the dressing table, brushing her hair. Something familiar, a vague association, was threatening to break through to the surface. Jess was lying on the bed behind her. His image was reflected in the mirror. The room was strange to her, and at the same time there was something familiar about it, some association she could not yet place.

She remained motionless, holding the brush. It was possible, she thought, to imagine this as a place where your familiar world ended, as situated at its extreme boundary—at the beginning of another world. If you entered this world, you left behind everything you used to be. Here love, as you had always imagined it, ended. Here your most vulnerable desires came to an end. Here the first signs of your undoing became visible.

If only she knew what it looked like outside, these anxious feelings could be dispelled. For the association was not merely with the room, but with what she imagined to be outside.

She did not take in anything Jess was saying. She remained absolutely motionless.

Then she knew, all of a sudden. While she was standing by the dressing table, it came back to her. This room reminded her of the hotel room she had been in one night years before—when rising from the cooling sheets she had decided that that was it, thus far and no further.

The irony of it all, she thought.

Jess took her in his arms, but tonight she was unable to meet him joyfully.

She slept fitfully. She dreamt unremittingly—there was a name she could not recall, it recurred repeatedly and in various awkward forms.

At last the sun rose. It shone in at their window. She stood looking out on the little town for the first time. It was different from what she had imagined during the night, as was to be expected.

She turned away from the window. There was a metallic taste in her mouth and nose, as if she had been walking a long way along a railway track.

Klaarte lay before her in the bright light of day, a tiny, picturesque dorp. They spent a pleasant day there and departed late in the afternoon, travelling on in a northeasterly direction.

CHAPTER 20

THEY DROVE in a northeasterly direction, towards the Eastern Transvaal. At dusk they reached the Dis Al Motel, where they had tea in the lounge. There was a large painting on the wall depicting Mabalel and the crocodile, painted by the proprietor. He had studied the painting techniques of Rubens in Belgium for seven years, he told them. And now, it seemed, the paintbrush had been replaced by a pistol—which he carried conspicuously in a holster on his hip. (To shoot any guest who dared eat in his bedroom, said Jess.) There were large animal skins on the ceiling. Antelope heads on the walls. In an adjoining room people played snooker—Afrikaner couples on the brink of suicide and dissipation. Homicidally depressed. Some national leaders came on television. Karolina and Jess went to their rondavel.

This part of the country had remained as she remembered it— rondavels, small wayside shops, subtropical vegetation—but it had a different feel, a different atmosphere from the city she had lived in for the past couple of years. She grew more reluctant to return to her life there, the further she travelled with Jess. With each additional stretch of the road that separated her from the harbour city and the undulating Natal midlands she felt her resistance growing.

They stuck to the route travelled by Adelia and Fernes. Karolina reconstructed the landscape alternately through the eyes of the child who had known it long ago, and through those of Adelia, who had only recently seen it for the first time.

At night Karolina and Jess lay in each other's arms in the ron-davel. They laughed and made love—each time, so it seemed, with greater intensity than before.

They spent a day visiting the Game Reserve. In a curio shop Karolina saw someone she thought she recognised. He was moving among row upon row of tiny ethnic dolls, decorated aprons, leather purses. He proceeded energetically among postcards, zebra skins (how was the widow doing, Karolina wondered), sundried fruit, painted ostrich eggs; he had a slight limp and a forbidding head. He moved among jewellery set with semiprecious stones, among beaded wooden spoons, among garments printed with animal motifs; no, she realised at last, he was not the person she had taken him for. Along the way Karolina and Jess saw a buffalo, a wildebeest, a kudu, a crocodile, a hippopotamus, a jackal, a few impala, and a few wart-hogs. They returned to the Dis Al Motel and drove back to Voor-spoed the next day.

As they approached the town, she had a sense of coming home. In the distance it lay serene in its hollow. It was hard to believe it was beset by conflict and strife. Hard to believe that Pol was down there somewhere (glass in hand), as well as Gert Els, the magistrate, Kieliemann and company, and hard to believe, at this distance, that this small town harboured all these lively and subversive souls.

"I am not going back to the city again," she told Jess.

"In that case you can come with me," he said.

"Will I be saved then?" she asked.

THE FOLLOWING DAY she went into the veld with Basil once more.

"What happened while I was away?" she asked.

"Plenty," said Basil, unemphatically, scraping sand off a stone.

"Such as?" she asked.

"There was a confrontation outside the post office between Gert Els and the township people. The people marched on the town with a string of demands which they presented to the town clerk."

"Was anyone hurt?" asked Karolina.

"No," said Basil.

"Where were you?" she asked.

"Oh," replied Basil impassively, "I was around."

"Were Beyers and Delarey there?" she asked.

"No," said Basil. "They've left."

"What will happen now?" she asked.

"We'll have to wait and see," said Basil, "the time is ripe."

LATER THAT WEEK she went to play snooker. First she had a drink in the ladies' bar, which was fairly empty since it was the middle of the week. Pol and some friends were having a low-keyed conversation in their corner. They could be plotting something, like everyone in this town seemed to be doing all the time. Too early in the evening still for the lusty singing of bawdy songs. She waited for him to appear at her left side.

"Would you say the time is ripe?" she asked once he was standing at her side, silent, conspiratorial, a drink on the counter before him.

"The lads in the township are very well organised these days," he replied (having first looked at her long and hard). "They won't allow themselves to be pushed around any longer. You should have been here on Monday when Gert Els almost went for them, right here, in the heart of town. Our very own captain had a hard time trying to restrain himself—it seems when it comes to blacks, the baton has a will of its own. He was furious with Sarel van Deventer, too, for wanting to negotiate. He threatened to throw the whole lot of them into the police van—Sarel as well."

"Who is Sarel van Deventer?"

"Beloved," said Pol gravely, "Sarel is our very own town clerk, our prince of commerce, our most prominent local entrepreneur, and the owner of the largest liquor outlet in town—the one across the road, next door to Chacka Brothers. Which means sixty per cent of his trade depends on black support."

Pol wiped the sweat from his face with a large, dark red handker-chief (a gift from his wife?). "This lad knows he is extremely vul-nerable to black consumer boycotts, so he begins to negotiate with the lads well in advance. He's had some experience of the persuasive

powers of these boycotts—it's hit him in the soft underbelly before."
(Karolina pictured a dark-haired, whiskered, go-getting, extravert-
ed, dynamic Sarel van Deventer, whose furry underbelly enclosed
metres of wet, entangled, bluey white intestines.)

Pol paused briefly. A light shudder passed through his body. He
cast a wily glance round the room.

"After the string of boycotts last year, Sarel advised the lads in
town to reconsider their options, and to consult with the ANC and
the township leaders. Some have begun to do so, but the diehards are
still holding out—just like our brave general of yesteryear."

He smiled sweetly at Karolina.

"Our very own captain is one of those who are unable to accept
the inevitable. The other lads are beginning to realise they should try
to get rid of him, but he is holding on for dear life. Now he's feeling
threatened on both sides, and that makes him even more unpredictable. He tends to go straight for the balls every time. Personally I
have absolutely no desire to poke my nose into his affairs," Pol said.

A slight tremor went through his body.

"I shudder to think of what this lad might do in a rash moment,"
he said, "if he were caught unawares. He has openly threatened the
township people—he has sufficient fire power to blow them all to
hell and gone, and if they should cause trouble in this town or anywhere else, he would not hesitate for a single moment to do so. He
grew purple with rage and frustration when they turned up here on
Monday morning."

"What are their demands?" asked Karolina.

"An ambulance and social workers in the township, a doctor at
the clinic, the recognition of a registered trade union at the munici-
pality: the usual things."

Pol began to hum softly to himself, his moist eyes scanning the
room furtively.

"What do you see?" asked Karolina.

"'Siena, my Siena, appears before my ey-es,'" Pol began to sing,
softly, insinuatingly.

Karolina looked around too, but failed to see anyone but the regulars. (Pol was of a naturally restive disposition—an attribute he had in common with Fernes Ramirez. Two very different people living at opposite ends of the world, sharing a single characteristic: an extreme restlessness of spirit.)

"Just tell me this," said Karolina, "What part do Beyers and Delarey have in organising the township people?"

"The lad who did most of the work," said Pol, "was disposed of recently—but this is just between you and me. You know all about it," he added.

"The man in the pickup truck," said Karolina, "the man who was killed in the accident?" (The attentive corpse.)

Pol nodded gravely. He nodded and nodded—a protracted nod.

Karolina gazed deep into his eyes, trying to fathom what their watery depths might hold. They looked at each other in silence for a while before Pol spoke. "Beyers and Delarey—the people's own travelling players," he said, "are in fact a wee bit too flamboyant for this area. They have, in truth, more important arenas of action. It's a case of overlapping interests. That's the reason they come here. And—in the case of Beyers—arrogance."

"You mean the woman?" asked Karolina.

Once more Pol nodded in silent affirmation.

"But who's the husband?" asked Karolina, remembering the long-suffering husband who had been by her side at the performance, and who sometimes sat over his untouched beer in the lounge next door, his broad, lonely back turned on the world. The man who—according to Basil—took his beautiful wife's infidelity like a man of breeding.

"The husband in question," said Pol, "is our very own town clerk, Sarel van Deventer."

IN HER ROOM Karolina reflected on the man she had thought she recognised among the ceremonial aprons and the leather artefacts in the curio shop. The nightly visitations by so many people she had known, male and female, continued, but with less urgency than before, when she had first arrived in this town.

Lovers, friends, relations still reported at night under various guises, the purpose of their appearance divergent, their schemes unfathomable. Some presented themselves repeatedly, an annoying regularity about their visits. Among these was the man who had courted her years before—the one who had been so little capable of love even then (she dreamt they were travelling by bus, she left a powder-blue necklace behind). Among those she had loved both her unrequited loves returned constantly. One of these would invariably appear in the company of a more desirable woman; the other was usually severe, rejecting, disapproving. As if she could not let go of them, but was still attempting to bind them to her by means of a dream, only to be thwarted anew every time. With the occasional glorious, shocking exception that left her confused and filled with longing the next morning. But more disconcerting was the gratification of desire from a more unexpected source. When it involved someone she did not care to associate with. When it happened to be Gert Els, or Kieliemann, or an acquaintance of no particular consequence. It was strange that erotic gratification would so often be linked in her dreams to the improbable, the unwelcome, the unthinkable even.

All of which served to add interest to Karolina's nights.

KAROLINA WANTED to know from Jess where his interest in Buddhism came from. She wanted to know what the Buddhist view of suicide was. She wanted to know how he wanted to live his life.

Buddhism was not the single most important content of his life, he said. He was no follower, he was not committed to the Buddhist—or any other—teaching, he merely valued it as an attitude to life. He had recently been more attracted to Zen than to Tibetan Buddhism—Zen seemed more attractive as a way of life. But in essence he had lapsed from every teaching.

Buddhism would not condone suicide, he said. Trying to escape from suffering was not the right way to endure it. This would merely add to the suffering in the next birth.

He pondered the third question before replying to it. She was cradled in his arm. The heavy, cream curtains stirred in the wind. Outside the light was immodestly crisp. The approaching autumn made a new, unfamiliar appeal to Karolina, and yet evoked old meanings. It brought with it pleasant as well as unpleasant associations.

Jess gave a little laugh. "Yes," he said. "How I would like to live. With an empty head—*and* with awareness."

They listened to the clear birdsong outside.

"And yet I have a liking for novels, for instance," he said, "in which the characters are constantly driven from one incident to the next, without necessarily knowing what it is that is driving them. That irrational, helter-skelter movement from one disaster to the next appeals to me immensely."

"Is it because you are that way inclined yourself?" asked Karolina.

Jess laughed again. He reflected briefly. "Perhaps because it mirrors my own lack of equanimity. Perhaps this is what attracts me in Buddhism too. It provides a way of coming to terms with the disquiet within myself. Something like that."

IN HER RELATIONSHIP with Jess, Karolina was coming to realise that she had no way of reading the graph of her desire, she had little insight into the conditions that made her reach out to Jess or that caused her to hold him at a distance.

Jess was hard to pin down. Sometimes he was absent. (Small wonder he should feel himself attracted to a teaching that emphasised the here and now.) How much of himself did he withhold in their daily interaction? He would sit there facing her, he would spread his legs, the furry (bronze) stomach contour visibly curved and powerful—sexually potent—beneath the shirt. But there was an air of reserve about his head, an indication of something that cautioned him to reticence and distance.

She considered him a strange person. He was attracted to Buddhism, he was in touch with his feelings, he valued dreams, yet in his choice of career he occupied himself with economic theory. With money; with the objective quantification of material commodities.

She did not know what to make of the curious blend of aloofness and accessibility in Jess, since during their lovemaking he opened up to her, he dropped his defences.

How very strangely they were lined up against each other. Since it was at these times, during their lovemaking, when it was expected of her to be fully there, that she tended to slip away most easily, as if she were losing control of her very presence. Of the devices that served to keep her present. No, it was not quite like that. She was indeed present. Intensely present. In his embrace every single one of her senses was keenly aware. But when she had to speak, when she was required to line up her very self against him, when she had to meet him with words, please him in the way he pleased her, she had little sense of personal self—she became a reflection, her mouth involuntarily repeating the words he uttered. She did not object to this—she merely found it strange.

IT WAS IMPOSSIBLE to think of her sister without thinking at the same time of her mother, or to think of her mother, and not of her sister. The two of them had been so profoundly attached, so closely linked, had loved each other so deeply.

At some moment her sister must have realised that she would have to lock away these overpowering feelings if she were ever to detach herself from the mother. She must have realised it was an absolute precondition for establishing her own life, independent of the mother. From that point onwards every stone, every lifeless rock, would serve as a repository of that terrible, displaced love. Of the terrible love of the mother for the child, of the child for the mother.

Their mother had not been able to come up with a similar strategy, nor a similar defence.

CHAPTER 21

KAROLINA COMPLETED her research in the autumn. The time was ripe to return to the city. She had to return to wind up her affairs.

As she lay in Jess's arm, she questioned him about his life: about his work, about his former loves, about his family. He spoke of these things, and of many other things besides. She listened attentively. The light was changing gradually. It was growing cooler, the birds were singing more sweetly. The sky was growing more insubstantial. The brightness, the boundlessness, the transience of each day made her heart contract.

She had always liked this landscape. Everything about it was so very flat. It was such an understatement. There was something subtler, more underground about the way things were done here, whether by people or by insects. The sky over the city was different—less open, less ephemeral, the night sky more lurid. The light was different there—less radiant, the subtropical colours were lusher, more garish.

HER LIFE IN the city had not been marked by deep dissatisfaction, by recklessness or longing, envy or rage, but rather by a lack of desire.

What had become of her desire? She had relinquished it. She had harnessed it, she had kept it at bay. She had become a stranger to her own desire.

Until the day she formulated her research, packed her bags, and came here to study the survival strategies of a certain species of moth. She had come to find out how these moths survived in difficult environmental conditions. She had come after the moths and had ended up in the snooker room. She had ended up in Jess's bed.

Jess told her the story of Soen Sa Su Nim. His skin turned green from the shredded pine needles he had been subsisting on for close on a hundred days. When he became a Zen master at the age of twenty-three, his teacher's parting words to him were: You are now a free man. Do not speak for three years. You and I shall meet again after five hundred years.

She liked this story. She turned her head to the right and looked out of the window.

She turned her head to the left and looked at the depiction on the wall of lord Yama, death, against a black background of nonexistence. He is recognisable only by the forms of his ornaments and attributes, symbolising the energies by which human beings—and all other things—seemed to appear and disappear, a process without beginning or end.

Lying in the darkening room she looked at Jess's dark, warm face. She studied it for signs. She watched him as though her life depended on it. He stroked her body. He turned towards her. His face was open, warm, and gentle. Their faces were close together, they looked at one another as if each could not get enough of the other.

KAROLINA HAD a friend who always appeared in her dreams in the same way. This was someone she had cared about deeply. They had been close friends for a long time. Then something had happened; there had been a shift; there was not much contact between them any more. But even when they had still been close, Karolina had had dreams in which she was forsaken by this woman. She had denied Karolina in her dreams from the very beginning. Don't do it to me, Karolina would beg her tearfully, night after night. Always in vain. In every dream the woman came up with new schemes, new ways of tormenting and rejecting Karolina; there was always someone else she would prefer to her. Someone whose friendship was worth abandoning Karolina for. It was like the dreams in which one of her two unrequited loves would always appear in the company of a more desirable woman.

JESS SAID: "I do not want to have to suppress my feelings!" (This he said deep into a Free State night.)

"Then don't," Karolina said, "don't do it then!"

BASIL WOULD point out things to her in the veld: Look! There were always new things to see. They looked at them together. They spent many afternoons sitting together in his spacious, cool room in Mr. Quiroga's house in the upper part of town. It was situated diagonally opposite the Look Ahead Home that had served as a refuge and shelter for unmarried mothers and orphans in the fifties.

She helped Basil to stick labels on the small storage bags. After four months every available shelf in his room was crammed with these bags, each containing a different, more unlikely substance. Among them were a variety of plants, roots, flowers, seeds, leaves, berries; finely ground, powdered land shells and stone shards; insects and spiders; a variety of crystals and elements (such as a shapeless chunk of sulphur—hard, brittle, yellow; tasteless and odourless—that emitted a brief, clear violet flame when Basil ignited it, and that was shrouded in dense, acrid fumes immediately afterwards). There was a variety of glass jars on the large table. One of these contained a fairly large spider (a four-lunged spider, genus *Orthognatha*), that Basil was preparing a tincture from. The finger root hung ever motionless in another jar. She would stare at it in unceasing fascination. Even now it looked more like a finger than like the root of a plant. A finger that had lain in water for a long time. She remembered the morning she had found it in the veld. A pointer.

He would be staying on for another month or so, said Basil. Then he would go back to the Cape. He had been doing it this way for a long time: returning here at two-yearly intervals to assist Mr. Quiroga and to learn from him.

She gazed out of the window. She sighed. What would she do without the daily excursions into the veld with Basil? How could she part from him? (Or from Pol, or the snooker room?) Her determination grew. She would not return to live in the city if she could help it.

"Where does this finger point to, Basil?" she asked him one afternoon.

Basil looked up at the finger, he was down on his knees on the floor, rearranging some cardboard boxes.

"That finger points to the west," he said.

To the west, where Karolina could see the sun going down this afternoon in bloody, fiery splendour, in extraordinary magnificence.

CHAPTER 22

AS AUTUMN approached, Karolina and the Kolyn fellow danced together ever more effortlessly. Their conversation between dances was as disjointed as ever (Karolina would gaze over his shoulder frequently at the shifting positions of the stars in the night sky). But with each passing week their footwork was more secure, their movements more coordinated as they became increasingly attuned to each other. They stunned and shocked their fellow dancers, they teased and gratified them, they laid bare the hidden possibilities of every dance.

During this season Karolina danced like a woman who was at times provocatively insinuating her love, at times openly displaying it, and at times concealing it at all cost. Her movements were steeped in desire, in anticipation and fulfilment. They were suffused with love, they were unbearably seductive. She did not hold back—within the range of what the context offered, she gave it all she had.

The Kolyn fellow, still wearing ankle sneakers and short pants, never let her down. His calf muscles were taut, but his dripping, expressionless face betrayed nothing of the effort he was putting into it. This season represented an unprecedented culmination for him as well. They seemed to move across the floor effortlessly, Karolina's body arched backward in a sensual curve, her hair all but sweeping the floor.

At first they still made small talk outside on the stoep between dances. He spoke of the effects of the drought, of fungal infestations in onions, of the curtailment of breeding programmes, of ways to combat shrinking profits, of aid schemes, and of desperate government measures. Karolina paid scant attention to this, sounding him out now and then about the latest reports from the township, or about the exploits of reservists and marauding gangs in the district. The Kolyn fellow invariably had news of some sort, for he was constantly travelling across the area. At times Karolina was convinced he was a police informer, or god knows what, something along those lines, but it seldom upset, surprised, interested, or inhibited her.

But as the positions of the celestial bodies gradually changed with the changing seasons, they fell increasingly silent between dances. They drank their orange squash and they dreamt, or they stared before them in silence—too spent, or too completely reconciled, or too enraptured by the dance to bother about words any longer.

Then the music would start up once again (the orchestra had become increasingly attuned to this particular couple, they played more purposefully than before). The other dancers, too, took their cue from them—as though a certain standard had been set against which to gauge their own performance, and to which they might aspire. And from the corner of the eye, unobtrusively, everybody would watch for the peaks, for those moments when the sensuousness ran like electric current through the air—when everything was just right, when all came together in perfect congruence, the music and the night, and the singular pair would send a collective wave of vicarious pleasure through the gathering.

Those rare moments, when Karolina became a reed, a cord, a willow, a snake, a flame, a burning torch, a witch. When she entered a narrow tunnel, and emerged at the other end (unscathed). When she and the Kolyn fellow became one flesh, a single resolve, a single writ, a single history.

In this way Karolina's extraordinary gift came into its own that season.

About twenty-five pairs of eyes, besides those of Lieutenant Kieliemann, Pol Habermaut, and the magistrate, followed her and the Kolyn fellow.

While the dance was in progress, these three would show up regularly in the doorway leading to the ladies' bar; they appeared in turn and at irregular intervals, they stayed briefly, or lingered—each with a different end in view.

Sometimes Karolina was aware of these appearances, more often she was not. She knew by this time what Pol and Kieliemann were about, but the magistrate remained a menacing presence, a closed book, a hidden link in a missing chain. He was a man who pissed a forked stream of acrid, yellowish green urine (foamy as beer); who likewise spoke with a forked tongue, who had an aversion to soiling his hands, whose genital and anal sweat smelt sweet, and to whose secret, shrouded life Pol had made no more than a furtive allusion. And in whose acid yellow, steaming jet (among other things) Basil had long—unbeknownst to her—discerned the violent end he was to come to.

THE SNOOKER ROOM was a seasonless space. When you entered it, the season no longer mattered. Neither did the time of day or night, nor the position of the celestial bodies, nor destiny and suffering, nor the inexorable course of the world out there. (Though all of these elements acted on the collective psyche of those present.) Here you entered a cosy, hermetically sealed space, disconnected from your hang-ups and worries, from the oppressive rhythms of daily living.

Gert Els came here regularly for inspiration, for a final boost that would enable him to put his scheme into operation; Tonnie de Melck had lost his head here nine weeks ago. Karolina had occasionally had an urge in here to dance on the green surface of the table—without her clothes, in an attempt to discover something about herself, to regain something she had lost.

Basil continued to be a sobering influence at her side. Whatever pronouncement he made—on the colour or odour of a person's urine, or the texture and substance of the seminal fluid, on the position and temperature of the genitals, or on the nature of the dreams, phobias or hidden impulses of those present—she could use as a reliable indicator for navigating a course through the dense room, for facilitating negotiations round the snooker table, and as a reliable barometer of the general state of mind of the other players.

She continued to admire these powers of Basil's, though she had long since stopped speculating on the precise nature of the source— his knowledge was drawn from so many sources—he relied upon in making any particular pronouncement.

ON A FRIDAY evening in autumn, during the sixteenth week of her stay, Karolina and Basil decided on a game or two of snooker. Jess had gone away for a couple of days to visit friends, she had not wanted to go with him, she felt the time had come to wind up her field work.

At first she sat a little halfheartedly beside Basil on the cane seat underneath the kudu head. But gradually the room filled up, there was an increase of laughter and talk, and she gave herself up to the mood of merrymaking. She liked the place. Everybody was there tonight: Kieliemann, Boet Visagie, Frikkie Visser, the teachers Abel Kriek and Tiny Botha, Balls Baluschagne in the opposite corner, the doctor with the limp, a few reps and salesmen, even the elder De Melck brother was back on the scene. (He seemed thinner, older, greyer. He was blond, too, but not in the same way as Tonnie had been.)

She watched the players at the snooker table. She studied their various expressions as they bent over the table to play a shot. The position of the fingers, the twist of the lips, the expression of an eye: grim or flustered, strained or nonchalant. Basil moved with his usual natural grace and serenity (he had a remarkably fine aim); Kielie-mann was somewhat more fanatical than usual, though his expres-sion remained impassive throughout.

Midway through the evening Gert Els suddenly appeared. The moment he entered Karolina felt her stomach contract with uneasy anticipation. She was aware of Basil becoming watchful as well. As usual, Gert Els had entered by the back door. (She could not recall ever having seen him in the ladies' bar.) Fortunately he seldom stayed long, as a rule he would come here to round up Kieliemann and company, to muster them for some kind of forceful action, a raid or something—frequently with barely concealed impatience, his entire body visibly prepared for action.

He seldom played snooker, but tonight was to be an exception. She had seen him play once or perhaps twice before, usually no more than a couple of rounds, before girding his loins once more for some disciplinary action. If ever she had seen a man permanently poised to strike, it was Gert Els.

Neither she nor Basil had ever felt like playing with him, or even being in the snooker room while he was there. So they went to the ladies' bar. She would remain there until he left.

The magistrate was sitting in his corner. He was not laughing tonight, he was sucking at the rim of his glass, not responding to his two companions. She knew Pol was there, at his usual table in the farthest corner across the room, behind her to the right. He was singing away with his friends; his sonorous bass had sounded up quite early in an exuberant military song. Judging by the inflexions of his voice and the suggestive emphasis of certain syllables of the refrain, an unusual slant was being given to the military theme.

Karolina and Basil had a whisky at the bar counter while they waited for Gert Els to finish his game and go off into the night with dark intent.

"Why should he come here to spoil our game," said Karolina.

Basil shrugged. When he had finished his drink he said he was going outside for some fresh air.

Not long afterwards, Pol appeared at Karolina's left side. They greeted each other.

"Have you any idea why Gert Els is hanging out here tonight?" she asked. "He doesn't usually stay this long. What is he up to?"

Pol gazed at her for a long time. Wiped the sweat from his brow with a large maroon handkerchief.

"Personally," he said, "I have not the faintest idea why that lad should find himself here tonight."

He took a great swig from his glass, then looked Karolina over, his head askance.

"And personally," he said, "I have not the least desire to know what he has up his sleeve."

Once more Pol's oily clamminess suggested something to her of the furry pelt of an animal adapted to prolonged and easy submersion in water.

"I have absolutely no desire tonight," said Pol, "to pollute my personal consciousness with the presence of that lad."

"I can subscribe to that," said Karolina.

Basil came in again.

"Is he still playing?" Karolina asked.

Basil paused at the door for a moment.

"Yes," he said.

Pol said good night; Karolina and Basil remained at the bar counter. Karolina half expected to see Jurie Beyers occupying the same space at the counter as on the night of Tonnie de Melck's death, when he had sat there with his elbows on the table and his fingers covering his face. She gazed at the large zebra skin displayed on the wall. She thought of the widow. She thought of Tonnie de Melck. She thought of Frans Roeg sitting alone at a table in the dark on the stoep of the hotel. Much has happened here, she thought.

She rose to leave, but sat down again as she looked at Basil's face.

"What's wrong?" she asked.

"There's going to be trouble," he said curtly.

"In that case I'm leaving right now," said Karolina, rising again. "I must get my bag in there."

As she entered the snooker room, Gert Els was leaning forward, taking careful aim. The mood had changed around the snooker table. There was none of the easygoing merriment any more. She could sense it straight away, it made her skin crawl. The other players were lined up round the table. Nobody dared to speak. They were waiting for Els to play his shot.

Gert Els was leaning forward, about to shoot, an expression of grim determination at the corners of his mouth; a grimace almost, the upper lip drawn away slightly, exposing the teeth. The large, pale hand, fingers spread on the green surface of the table, seemed to have an independent existence, to squat there like some lowly creature. The white ball lay against the tip of the cue, and in front of the red one, the black ball.

Karolina stood looking on reluctantly, involuntarily, riveted to the spot. Gert Els had the same bluish green pallor as on the night Tonnie de Melck had died. Basil was right, the blood seemed to run in his veins like cold water. (Did his head feel packed in ice, his innards all knotted up?)

He played his shot. It was a lousy shot. He straightened up slowly. Only then did Karolina become aware of the voices outside. The sound of a great many voices was growing more distinct. The others heard it, too. Gert Els stood frozen, listening, his jaw clenched tightly.

Karolina snatched up her handbag from under the cane seat and made for the exit as fast as she could, through the ladies' bar, through the lounge, through the baroque reception area. Basil was nowhere to be seen. She did not feel up to whatever might be coming next.

Outside, a police vehicle—its light flashing—was already drawn up in front of the hotel entrance, and another was parked at the corner. A group of black people was gathered in the street between the two vehicles, and facing them was Gert Els. How had he managed to get there so fast—had he come through the window of the snooker room, was there a secret doorway somewhere?

Karolina moved closer, since she recognised two of the three black men directly facing Els. One of them was the man whose brother had been murdered, who had told the story of how he had fled from Standerton here in the street by the very same flashing yellow light, and the other was Philemon Mhlambi, the man from whose house in the township Gert Els had emerged.

Karolina moved closer still. Her heart seemed to be beating somewhere in her throat. Gert Els stood with his back to the hotel, immediately in front of the brightly-lit windows of the snooker room.

Kieliemann and Buytendach were almost directly behind him. Boet Visagie, Frikkie Visser, a few other policemen Karolina had never seen before and two young reservists completed the semicircle to his left.

Inside the snooker room and the ladies' bar people were visible—in silhouette—before the open windows. Karolina thought she could make out Pol's dark figure, glass in hand, half hidden by a curtain, and the two teachers and the doctor at a window. (All of them waiting in the wings?)

Behind the three people directly facing Gert Els a group of black people huddled together. The man who had told the story of his escape was speaking to Els. He was using the same careful, neat Afrikaans. There was a steadily growing silence. The flashing light of the police vehicle had been turned off.

Gert Els stood motionless. By the light of the street lamp his face was clearly visible. His gaze was cold, his jaw clenched, the baton tapped regularly on the thigh. He looked dreadful, his eyes were sunken in their sockets, his face bluish. (A sensation of something live stirring in his gut?)

"We have come once more to bring the charge that the captain would not receive this morning," the man said calmly.

"I am not accepting it," Els said. (His tongue heavy and cold.)

Philemon Mhlambi stepped forward suddenly. "You have to accept it!" he said, and held out a piece of paper to Gert Els.

Els stepped forward too, and slapped Mhlambi's face with the side of his hand, causing him to stagger to one side and fall down. Then he got hold of the man's shirt and jerked him halfway back on his knees, ripping open his shirt as he did so. Then he kicked him in the stomach.

Philemon Mhlambi folded over on his knees.

A sigh, like a wave, went through the bystanders.

The other man spat a well-aimed, contemptuous jet on the ground before Els's feet.

Whereupon Gert Els whipped out his service pistol and aimed it at him.

"You have three minutes," he said in a low voice, "to get out of here. Or I'll blow you all away."

The man remained motionless before him. So did the crowd behind him.

Philemon Mhlambi was still down on his knees. He was clutching his stomach. Karolina could see blood gushing from his nose. Basil had moved in from somewhere, he was easing Mhlambi carefully into a prone position.

Gert Els still had the pistol trained on the man in front of him. Some of the people at the back of the crowd began to mutter; the crowd started breaking up, people at the back began moving off halfheartedly. The police were keeping a close watch on them.

The next moment Karolina heard a tremendous bang, like an explosion—in the snooker room—and the sound of shattering glass. People screamed, scattered apart, ran off in all directions. Karolina saw the curtains catch fire and rise up in the wind, she was running too, to the other side of the street.

Basil remained on his knees beside the man, two black men at his side. Inside the hotel a fire was raging. Smoke began to emerge from the windows.

People rushed out through the front entrance of the hotel, choking on the smoke. From behind the building people were rushing out too, they had probably escaped through the dining room.

Where was Pol? What was happening to the painted panels! Karolina ran across the street, back to Basil, still kneeling at Mhlambe's side, but the heat of the fire was almost unbearable there.

"Basil!" she cried. He looked up briefly, motioned to her to move off.

Behind him, inside the snooker room, she saw the snooker table magnificently aflame—it was blazing away relentlessly, determinedly.

She ran to the entrance of the hotel.

"Pol!" she cried. "Pol!" she heard herself calling, in a voice she did not recognise as her own.

People were staggering out through the front entrance one by one, along with the billowing smoke. She saw the elder De Melck brother, one or two reps, men and women she had noticed in passing in the ladies' bar, but still there was no sign of Pol.

"Oh, God," said Karolina, wringing her hands. She picked up the sound of the fire engine with some relief; the town's ambulance drew up across the road. The fire brigade arrived, spilling its crew.

At the same time, to Karolina's relief, the figure of Pol Habermaut appeared in the doorway, so completely covered with soot as to be almost unrecognisable.

Karolina ran towards him. Some of the firemen also rushed up to support him, since he was barely able to manage another step. She stood a few metres away from him, in the glow of the blaze. The heat was incredible. People were crowding behind her, locals who had come to look at the fire.

"Pol!" she called, reaching out to him.

But he must have suffered serious injury and shock; underneath the layer of soot covering his face (how did his shirt and trousers come to be so black?) his cheek was covered in blood, and there was blood on his arm too; flying glass, perhaps.

He had a glazed stare. He seemed to be looking at something on the other side of the street that no one else could see—something beyond the crowd. He was supported by a fireman on either side.

"I shudder . . ." he said feebly, but he was unable to complete the sentence. He collapsed into the arms of the two men. They took him off to a waiting ambulance.

Some firemen emerged, bearing people on stretchers. As another pair of them went by, she discerned the magistrate lying prone on a stretcher. Like Pol, he was barely recognisable, his clothes were burnt black, he was covered with soot, but it seemed he had not come off as lightly as Pol.

He lay motionless. His eyes were not quite closed. There was blood at the side of his head, and a trickle of blood at the corner of his mouth. One hand lay limply across his chest. The hand was dirty, the nails were dirty—it seemed as though he had been clawing at something. She heard a fireman tell of a burning beam that had come down on some of the injured. They were waiting for the ambulance to return. Karolina could not stop looking at the magistrate. She could not take her eyes off him. She had never seen him at such close range before. She had never spoken to him. And yet he seemed so very familiar. She felt she knew him well, as though during all these years he had occasionally sat at her bedside at night, never once disclosing the purpose of the visit. Gert Els's silent accomplice. The man in her dream: down on his knees, lecherous, hopelessly, indecently, obscenely so.

CHAPTER 23

KAROLINA AND BASIL went to see the hotel the next morning. It was a clear day, but the sky above the town was still dense with smoke.

Small groups of people hung about. The building was still emitting heat, despite the wet soot and ashes. The front part seemed to have been most extensively damaged. The snooker room was unrecognisable, even though the walls were still standing. From the street it looked as if the baroque staircase and the reception area had remained intact.

Karolina stood gazing at the hotel for a long time. They walked round the back. It was hard to tell from this distance what damage had been done to the painted panels.

"How badly was the man injured?" she asked Basil.

"He'll be okay," said Basil.

Afterwards they went out into the veld, but Karolina could not concentrate. She followed Basil mechanically. Later they sat under the willow tree. They had tea from the Thermos and ate a sandwich.

"What will happen to Gert Els now?" she asked. "Surely everyone saw him kick that man."

"It shouldn't be too hard to make out a case of provocation," said Basil. "It all depends whose evidence is used."

"Maybe this will be his undoing," said Karolina.

She gazed into the distance, the horizon so changed today. A cloud of smoke was still visible over the town.

They walked back to town along the direct route, not the one past the cemetery, which she preferred. Her legs seemed too weak for a long walk today.

She went into the chemist's shop towards the end of the morning to buy a reel of film and some vitamin pills.

Had they perhaps heard anything about the condition of the lawyer, Mr. Habermaut, and the magistrate, she asked one of the assistants after some hesitation. They were injured in the fire last night, she added.

The woman put Karolina's tablets and the film into a paper bag, took the money from her, counted out the change. Both men had been admitted to the hospital at Volksrust, she said (casting a mistrustful glance at Karolina). Mrs. Habermaut had been in the chemist's shop this morning, and she had told them that her husband was in a stable condition.

"And the man who was kicked?" she asked.

"The black?" the woman asked.

Karolina nodded.

"No, Madam, I wouldn't know about that," the woman said, fixing her gaze on a customer behind Karolina.

THE DAMAGE to the hotel turned out to be less extensive than it had seemed at first glance. The snooker table—where the petrol bomb had landed—was of course damaged beyond repair. The green surface had immediately started to burn fiercely. A young black man had apparently come up behind the building, and had hurled the homemade petrol bomb into the snooker room through an open side window. The wooden bar counter in the ladies' bar had also been destroyed. But the painted panels in the dining room and the baroque staircase and reception area merely needed a thorough cleaning.

Pol and the magistrate survived, although both—the magistrate in particular—had sustained serious burns. A case of culpable homicide was being brought against Gert Els. Karolina and Basil heard all about it in town over the following week—in the cafés, in the chemists' shops, at the general dealer's, at Steyn and Sons' Stationery.

Towards the end of the week Karolina learnt (at the chemist's shop, once again) that Pol had been transferred to the local hospital.

She sat on one side of Pol's bed, and Mrs. Pol Habermaut, made flesh at last after all these weeks, sat on the other. She was a lively, sympathetic woman, who clearly went about her business in this town with great energy and enthusiasm. Two half-grown children were also present at his bedside, they seemed amazingly untroubled and unimpaired.

In the bed, at the centre of all this, lay Pol, swaddled in bandages like a mummy. His hands were spread in blessing over the entire company, like Jacob of old.

KAROLINA DREAMT prolifically the whole week. (Jess was not back yet.) Young children appeared in her dreams. She dreamt she was feeling abandoned and lost. She had dreams of intense panic. In one of these dreams she was more forcefully confronted with her own death than was possible when she was awake. She dreamt she was holding Jess's penis, it was covered with a cloth. It was firm as a rod. She could not close her thumb and her middle finger round it. She dreamt of her own arousal. Outside it was raining, she heard, a cool and untimely, but comforting autumn rain. She woke up and realised it was not rain, but wind that had come up and was stirring the autumn leaves.

SHE NEVER HAD another chance to dance with the Kolyn fellow. They ran into each other in town one more time, shook hands solemnly, and went their separate ways.

KAROLINA ASKED Basil to take a photograph of her outside the ruined hotel. She wanted to send it to Adelia. How she regretted not having had a picture of herself in front of the hotel taken earlier, before the fire. Or of Adelia and Fernes on the hotel stoep. But who would have thought then that it would not always remain as it was.

She wrote to Adelia, telling her what had happened. Their letters crossed over the Atlantic Ocean, she received a letter from Bogotá a few days later.

Adelia said that she was making a painting of the four of them dancing in the dry bed of the spruit. She had been inspired by the painted panels, the figures were tiny and the landscape was vast. She wrote that she was putting in everything—the tufts of grass, the stones, the dead crabs, the land shells, the insects, the butterflies, the moths (for Karolina), the hares, the food they had eaten, the blankets, the willows, the clouds gathering at the horizon. At the bottom of the picture she drew the notes of the music they were dancing to. She was doing it in the colours of the veld: ochres, pinkish browns, faded greens, indigo blue for the sky. It was a huge canvas, she said. A variation on the theme of the picnic on the grass, but in the heroic tradition of Altdorfer, or of those baroque paintings in which the figures are dominated by the immensity of sky and landscape.

You must come to visit us, there is much here that would interest you, she wrote.

"I'LL BE LEAVING here within a week," Karolina told Jess in late autumn, during the seventeenth week of her stay in Voorspoed. "I think I have found what I was looking for here. I should be able to make something of it in my research."

Something my father would have been proud of, she wanted to add, but she did not.

They were sitting in the Rendezvous Café. Jess remained silent for a while.

"You know how important it is to me that we should be together," he said.

She nodded. "It's important to me, too," she said.

This he said in the café and in broad daylight. His hand—freckled, covered with small, rusty red hairs—rested on the book with the red cover (which he had not had with him for a long time). His gaze veiled, his eyes averted, his voice somewhat hesitant. The tea less drinkable than ever.

But at night, when the moon was like a moist eye in the middle of the velvety sky, when his body glowed by its pale light, when its surface was so hot that it burnt her hands, Jess would draw her close to him, he would hold her tight in his embrace and he would pour a flood of words in her (receptive) ear: he loved her, he said, and he would say it over and over again, that he loved her.

KAROLINA RETURNED to the hot, humid city. She wrote up her research there, she packed her bags, and left the city without regret.

THEY RETURNED to the town once or twice a year—sometimes she went there with Jess, and sometimes Basil would accompany them. They took their meals in the dining room with the (restored) painted panels, she and Jess had tea at the Rendezvous Café. The snooker table in the renovated snooker room had been replaced by three pool tables. It was not as cosy as before, it had lost much of its former atmosphere. When Basil came to visit, he would stay with his teacher, Mr. Quiroga, so as to be initiated ever more deeply into the mystery of the remedies. Whenever they happened to be there at the same time, Karolina and Basil walked in the veld, much greener now after the rains. The sky would open up above her like a fan, wide, unending.

She paid regular visits to the cemetery. She went to see the grave of Tonnie de Melck, marked by an enormous granite monument. His name, the dates of his birth and of his death, and a text from the Bible were inscribed on it:

I have called thee by thy name. Thou art mine. (Isaiah 43:1)

All the better for Tonnie if these words should be true, Karolina thought.

And whenever she walked in the cemetery, under the delicate china-blue sky, whenever she walked among the graves, or sat on the small bench by the cypress tree, or looked at the new extension, she would always look out for the lovers—she looked out for them constantly, she never ceased to look for the lovers.

Ingrid Winterbach is an artist and novelist whose work has won South Africa's M-Net Prize, Old Mutual Literary Prize, the University of Johannesburg Prize for Creative Writing, and the W.A. Hofmeyr Prize. *To Hell with Cronjé* won the 2004 Hertzog Prize, an honor she shares with the novelists Breyten Breytenbach and Etienne Leroux. Her novels *To Hell with Cronjé* and *The Book of Happenstance* are also available from Open Letter.

Iris Marguerite Gouws, née Terblanche (1942–1998), was educated in the Free State and North West Province, and studied toward a BA in Fine Arts at the University of the Witwatersrand. She was an accomplished painter with a lifelong passionate interest in both art history and literature.

Open Letter—the University of Rochester's nonprofit, literary translation press—is one of only a handful of publishing houses dedicated to increasing access to world literature for English readers. Publishing ten titles in translation each year, Open Letter searches for works that are extraordinary and influential, works that we hope will become the classics of tomorrow.

Making world literature available in English is crucial to opening our cultural borders, and its availability plays a vital role in maintaining a healthy and vibrant book culture. Open Letter strives to cultivate an audience for these works by helping readers discover imaginative, stunning works of fiction and poetry, and by creating a constellation of international writing that is engaging, stimulating, and enduring.

Current and forthcoming titles from Open Letter include works from Argentina, Bulgaria, France, Greece, Iceland, Latvia, Poland, and many other countries.

www.openletterbooks.org